THE NIVIAN KING
Book 1

THE NIVIAN KING SERIES BOOKS

SELECT NONFICTION

THE NIVIAN KING
Book 1

PARIS TOSEN

Tosen Books

The Nivian King is a work of fiction.

Copyright © 2011 by Paris Tosen

ISBN: 978-1-926949-20-8

www.tosen.ca

Book design and cover by Paris Tosen

THE NIVIAN KING

A seed is in a continual state of birth. — Tulai Khan, inventor

Prologue

Live as a rolling wind.
— *old Seronian proverb*

EXPANSION AND contraction. Breath. Life's one true
dependent. The breaths of life: freedom and control.
The sacrifices for such intangibles are unique to
their environment and realm of sophistication.
Freedom is the slave; and control, the master. But
breath nor slaves can be kept for an eternity, and
without freedom there is nothing to control. Excess
freedom leads to a cannibalization that digests the
original purpose as a phosphorescent fire liquefies
shards of glacial ice. Freedom only exists because

control exists; and control is perpetuated from the grant of unlimited freedom. The breath is the swing. The scale of uncertainties of all possibilities.

The Versos, a doubly-twisted strand of realized existence in the cosmic pool, was the pendulum of Opus and Ora, the essences of freedom and control manifested in the opposing planets of Flamma and Ice; and had existed for tens of thousands of tios, measured in the eighteen-month halation of the cosmic seragon, Seranor. It was she who remained to remind the Kozotal and Nivians that the cosmic strand was pulled taut from their diametric functions.

Since the beginning, the flammic Kozotal, creationary beings of light residing in the first planet Mettadi-di Flamma, were the warmth and the direction to the Versos. Beyond their luminescence lay the realm of all that could be, and forever would be, the beauty of Opus. On the lowest planet, the twenty-third, ice born Nivians guarded Nivatasek-ande'ot. The realm of Nivata, as it came to be, was absolute control. It was the end of the strand. Beyond its frigid state lay total stillness.

Should either Opus or Ora exist as the greater force, the Versos would sway wildly and continue to bulge until it evaporated from obliterating radiation or snapped of cryonic temperatures that seized atomic motion. Opus and Ora provided the movements of halation.

Breath needed interaction to satisfy its purpose. Persistent motivation necessitated that interactivity between all things and ensured that the battle for one or the other, freedom or control, was not fought for one day nor was it stopped though there were times when all living things needed to be reminded of such inter-relatedness and dependencies.

It was inevitable that the bluish-skinned Nivians would extend their icy grip from planet Nivata to wring more power from what had been allotted to them and their inherent deficit needs. The nature of Nivians was of maximization, efficiency and corruption as determined as the liquid ice crystals circulating their inner pathways and feeding their existence.

Such instruments of movement to claim the better part was fought on Aquanomicus, the twelfth planet and now called Seranor for it was her enslaved body that made up the land masses. And her colossal serpentine seedling, Seragorn; caged and now intertwined, joined by mouth and tail to his mother. He was the originator of the ceramic Entan beings who were created with the four elements of Ceramico, Cora, Flamma and Arvano, and whose porcelan bodies were made to guard and keep the planet healthy. To keep Seranor and Seragorn living, and to ensure that Opus could maintain the balance in the Versos. Ora commanded the Morb and Cerbors, shelled clay monsters who were the doom of Entans.

Entans stood two meters tall, were gifted with smooth white porcelan skin and round eyes of uniform color, and the unlimited ability to learn except if filtered by their cerbinds: keeper of wills, thoughts and memories. Only a scarce number of entans were scarred or crippled in some way although many were found with imperfections and marks on their skin unlike the first generation who were capable of making their bodies transparent. Entan milk, blood, was white, thick and the energizer of life. Entans followed opus and were the free. Kozoty, descendants of Kozotal, were present to guide them. They were hybrids of porcelan and flamma with greater capacity for achievement. And it was the great Kozoty, Polinatimus Kalto, and his supporters who diffused the age long battle between the Serag, cleansers of the planet, and the Malkar, destroyers of beauty. Polinatimus banished the elemental Malkar from the plane wielding the power of Orbis Inigra and allowed planet Seranor to flourish.

Seronians adhered to three profound truths: Art, Philosophy and Flamma. What of truth? An illusion of actuality and a damnation of causality. The Flamma was the gift from the Kozotal. It was the bright fire that served all. Art was the reason for color and joy. And Philosophy, philosophy was food for creativity and pacifism. Together they formed the cornerstones of Seronian thought keeping the pendulum rhythmic and timely.

In the breath of the Versos, only one constant was true: interactivity. The greater the interactive force, the more dramatic the results. The more drastic the needs. Severity would so hear the inaudible cry of mother Seranor. Severity would come, as it always did, in its many, many disguises.

Chapter 1

LAW WAS the device of the phobic, politic the device of the suave, science for the agnostic, military of the vindictive – combined, they formed the four rules on the frozen planet Nivata; and home of the Nivian kingdom, masters of control and structure: non-believers in who the devices served. Masters of the rules.

All that was commanded by King Llinduus was waning, the military Generals no longer enforced his will choosing to follow those of his senior Advisory Commander, a handsome, orange-eyed Nivian twin determined to upset the cosmic balance, who now secretly controlled more than half of the one thousand three hundred Generals throughout the ice kingdom. It was the top of the seventh month that power had been shifting hands, and not only the King and his cohorts, but all Nivians were feeling its effects. Amana, the soon-to-be-dethroned King's daughter, had subsided her support for her father even since before his reign began to falter; she was of a refined devious beauty seductively involved in matters despite her recent birth to a seedling from an undetermined Nivian. She claimed it to be of senior Advisory Commander Zorath, but he knew of her secret mating with Commander Rascoth, his twin brother; Commander Zorath kept it quiet inside while focusing more intently on his strategic plan to usurp the power of the crown. He obsessed himself with it. Amana continued to play all sides thinking that he was unaware of her deception; his twin had indulged into his love affairs but remained loyal to Zorath's predictions up to this point; the current Generals went absent without notice of return; soldiers supported disruptions among the population; instability increased across the glacial peaks.

On the day of suspicion, Nahkli-li-Zorath, or Zorath as he was referred to by all those who recognized his superiority, had fixed all final preparations and now gazed across the site of his future kingdom from the wide balcony on the eastern face of the magnificent Battlekeep Kalimantan, a massive ice ship fixed in its position. Whites and greens with highlights of silver and blue colored the landscape and most things on the planet. Nivo, where the Nivian kingdom was commanded, was made of large bergs of snowy ice that floated together as gigantic cubes of blue coated in green slush. Kalimantan towered over all.

Ice commanded the greatest energies without defects or impurities and in its most fundamental composition was the complete disappearance of resistance — and total control. Perfection, it was believed, was made in cryogenic formation, the birthplace of all Nivians.

Nivata, the anchoring planet, was the frigid gate between absolution and evolution in the Versos. Its entire physical composition was of super conductive ice that allowed arvic transmission to flow without a deck of resistance feeding the invisible streams of arvicity that permeated the glacial planet; and nullifying the greed and lust of Nivians, perfect oratic beings with naqui milk, burning liquid ice blood transfused throughout their bodies; and designed to suck and harvest arvic energies.

Arvicity, magnetically resonating electrical pulse energy flooding the entire Versos provided all life's needs, and its transmission on the ice planet saturated the crystalline structures and particles far richer than the other two planets, Mettadi-di Flamma and Aquanomicus.

Kalimantan was situated upon an expansive ice plate extending farther than the eyes could see, with many structures at the top, as well as a probing keel that dove itself down into the icy aqua keeping it afloat as if a long arm reached into the planet's core and clutched its corius.

A SOFT and steady wind blew Zorath's long white hair so that it swung all to one side and exposed his handsome blue skinned face and rectangular-shaped eyes made of translucent orange. Piercing they were. Eyes of Nivian were all shaped the same but orange was the first of its kind on the planet. He shifted his long, well-developed body to the other side, the soft flexible ice armor suit glistened; then he silently removed a long silvery rod nearly one-and-a-half meters from front to end, fitted snugly into his sash, and held it out in his right hand into the wind.

A thick, black-chained necklace hung loosely around his neck falling to a square black piece. When his hair was whisked away, closer inspection revealed the detailed blue background on which a long, pointed white spike, tall and vertical, shot up to the dark sky and into forever. The spike and mark of the current King. The hand that now held fast the rod had a similarly designed black ring—but the markings on the rod bore no resemblance.

His eyes reflected the green-blue landscape certain that it would all soon be his to rule. Success was a certainty: Yes, he had known success his entire mature life. Control, he thought, was only the result of pervasive subliminal manipulation, and that was not a skill. It was a desire.

Zorath was constructed of a combination of desire and delicacy. He viciously sent his birth parents into the berg population to live among excess and entertainment when they refused to understand his ambitious demands preferring to obsess themselves with the absurdity of procrastination – the one commonality found throughout the bergs. Nivians mated frequently, powered by their hyper sex drives, but produced only one seedling.

He not only vowed to them but knew with such certainty that one day he would be a great king and all against him would falter against his magnificence. If there was an obsession he had, it was such a goal. Zorath never liked something controlling him and it was why the Versos and all of its cosmogony frustrated him to points of unrealistic self. Control was for the powerful and he could not accept anything less than absolute control. He felt the oppression against him, keeping him where he was but Zorath would fight this constant and never-ending force until he could subdue it in its entirety. He would eradicate it, corrupt it and swallow its power whole thereby satisfying his life's desire to be the controller and not the controlled.

Some considered Zorath an unusual Nivian. All Nivians were enchanted geniuses able to manipulate powerful arvicity, but Zorath had two immense differences among others: manipulation and passion. His ability to manipulate arvic flows were not the uniform methods inherent to Nivian naqui. It was thought that his second uniqueness, that of passion, tainted his arvic spells and caused strange and unpredictable fluctuations in his casting. This caught many off guard and earned him successive victories in battle to those who opposed him and to those he singled out as potential threats. Passion was the frayed weakness of Nivians who vehemently believed in control, structure and the four rules. The variability and fluctuation of action laced with this defect was considered to be the one true weakness, the death, of the blue-skinned beings.

ZORATH KNEW his so-called "defect" was the driver of his ambition and would recognize his first step into the cosmic pool. Once Nivata was his domain then he would invade and remove the will of Aquanomicus, protected by the two cosmic Seragons, and once that was accomplished planum Mettadi-di Flamma would freeze and the Versos would snap as a brittle glass releasing its life force into him. Though in his charged drive for resolution his camouflaged sight masked the true effects of his characteristic emotional flaw.

He heard the familiar jerking footsteps of his brother approaching from behind. Twins were the rarest of realities on Nivata. They were freak occurrences with unimaginable outcomes. It was then that he recalled what had driven him further into his determination, and deeper to his self; and farther from his Amana – his own naqui milk. A sour taste grew in the left corner of his mouth and temporarily caused his entire face to become tense and freeze in its position, then returned it once more to unseen agitation and neutrality.

"A resolution is due, brother," he said as he turned holding the rod and pointing to Rascoth.

Silvery scales made up Rascoth's shirt of armor. The king's mark, similar to Zorath's amulet, was engraved in the right breast. The long snow-green hilt of a *rader* sat coldly in the scabbard on his right hip. The length of the hilt matched that of the quattro-blade, blunt and lethal: enough to rip through any opponent. Rascoth's long hair flew openly along with his tunic in the airy breeze.

The wind's continued force shifted Zorath's hair momentarily shielding his face before revealing his charismatic smile. The air refreshed him. "Llinduus is weak, his forces are dispersed, and the crown is soon at hand — our hand, brother!"

"General Kulkithon informs me that the other generals will follow. Every one of them," replied Rascoth, brilliant white eyes, of nobility for certain, as a smile caught one corner of his mouth.

"Then all is set. The kingdom is ready and once Nivo is under our control," he paused slightly to look at the reaction to the words *under our control* then continued, "we will control all of Nivata and when all is set we will invade Aquanomicus and drain Seranor of all her defenses."

"And her seedling, Seragorn, will drown with her as will all entans," said Rascoth.

"The eternal struggle will vanish in our favor and the Kozotal will suffocate in stillness. And the cosmic lake shall congeal with the twist of my hand!" he said while slowly spinning the rod in one hand and watching it semi-hypnotize Rascoth who could not help from watching the white tip going round and round.

"We must take action today, brother. Timing and preparation are joined as one."

"Then prepare the others and find me in my chamber by the cut of the hour. And follow our plan closely."

"As all shall," Rascoth replied and turned his back to his twin. "As all shall," he said and then smiled coldly, looking with both eyes to the right at slight angle towards his brother as if the timer of a secret was about to elapse. Rascoth marched out.

THE ROUND chamber where Zorath comfortably sat in a supple snow couch, cast in green tinge, that form-fitted his body to every tiny nuance, was essentially barren except for evidence in sharp protrusions along various points in the room – technological controls and devices – and on tables of semi-transparent ice. Its minimalist design did not create the feeling of being behind closed walls. He thought an image and instantaneously a *guin*, a golden liquid contained by a barely visible glass, appeared in his left hand. He sipped gently and with each sip sank further into the recesses of his cerbind. All would soon be his and, once started, his plan could not be stopped. He already possessed *Seca*, the ancient rod of carving, the same device used as part of a set in the making of Aquanomicus, the planet now called Seranor after its birth mother.

As he continued to enjoy his guin and closed his eyes he drifted his cerbind into the safety of his trusted self.

"Have you called me one?" said a soft, soothing voice that resonated through the stale chilly air and warmed his ears pulling out his senses. It was Amana, the King's seedling and the one he foolishly loved: His wife. She radiated skin of arvic blue with glossed silver hair that ran down to her hips like the shape of a polished vase that wanted to be touched but held a degree of frailty. Her half-meter hair was tied tall today and she moved with a stalking sensual grace as she approached Zorath in her usual half-naked body that highlighted her voluptuousness and cracked his primal wall of protection. The room filled with her presence and pulled him from his space of safety.

"No. You haven't finished remobilizing," said Zorath, not able to express the emotion he wanted about the female he began to loathe. She had been the mother to his seedling, his first and only.

"But I feel as before, my handsome Commander," she replied in an erotic tone.

He swallowed all the yellowish drink at once, speaking flatly, "I was expecting my brother. Where is he?" He asked suspicious that his brother had deviated from the plan because of her. She was his dissolution.

"How can I know where he is? He does not inform me of all his desires."

"Enough, Amana! Why are you here?"

"Zorath, you haven't seen me often since the birth and it seems you and I have been apart for thirty tios."

He rose, adjusted his clothes calmly and assuredly then moved to the curved set of ice windows covering one entire wall of the room. His hand on the engraved silver rod with the white sphere on the end, for comfort. She could see him in the reflection.

"It seems many things have parted us," he said with a taste of regret in his voice.

"Not so many things," she replied, but she knew that he now suspected something between her and Rascoth though nothing conclusive was found; she made certain of that. She moved closer to him, close enough to be seen between him and his reflection in the window. She touched him on the shoulder; he stared hard outside to prevent a tear, but she knew that time was imperative and that she mustn't let him deviate from his plan as it would affect all that she had done and the future of her seedling.

"You have to promise me to relieve yourself of some of your future responsibilities when all is done," she said. "I fear your health has been weakened."

"I am never weak — never! And never fooled by any," he said reaffirming his state of cerbind. She had betrayed him, he was sure of it and had seen evidence from her translucency, but he loved her so much that he forgave her for it and didn't realize all else that had been forgiven and would soon discover. He also knew that she loved him from a certain perspective even she could not deny. Love was not as easily dissipated as it formed, even the cold love between Nivians. "And you are always beautiful, Amana. How is our seedling?"

"She is safe."

"Good."

"Your ways of self can be improved for success is not all that fills the air on Nivata."

"Time enough will come for improvement. We all can be improved." Looking at her as she looked through him into a blurry future.

"And my father?"

"Wait here while your father hands me a crown." He had regained his focus and once again removed her from his cerbind. "Destiny approaches us all and does not care our choice. You have despised of your father ever since he forced you to listen to me," he said directly.

"How did you know of that?"

"I can know certain things. I am Zorath, destined to succeed under all circumstances—all of them. I have loved you more than you could ever love me, but a single day has not passed where as much love was returned. Your love is but a purpose."

"Why not speak of this before?" she asked, unaware of his feelings now.

"Before what?" he said.

"Before today. Before now."

"Love does not require love to exist," said Zorath. "You are the foolishness in mine eyes. A reflection of a tender spot inside me." He looked into her eyes and then slowly closed them as he continued. "If there could be such a point I would measure it and extract it. But if it is my twin that you love more then I ask you to leave me and love him."

"You cannot know of my father's demands and how much they detain me and my emotions," she said in defense.

"Your emotions have lost their effects as you have of your way. When the crown has changed hands, I will cast out my brother and you will leave with him to live among the bergs. There you will learn to taste the pains I have tasted from your infidelity and his virility. Together you can serve one another well. I am sure."

"You cannot do this, Zorath. I have —"

"You have done nothing to prevent this. In fact, you have inspired it."

"I will not let you do this," she demanded.

"You will swallow it whole or die from my command."

Amana challenged his verse: "The command that I have given you. It is from my work that father has hailed you as a respected leader!"

"If not for that I would have slain you long before this day," he said, then manipulated his fingers casting a spell that held Amana fast to where she stood unable to speak or move. He approached her.

"And if not for my love I would have melted your flesh where you stand. It was not your beauty that made me love you. It was not that at all though you wear it well." He spoke slow to highlight his true intention fighting hard to hide his pain, turning and walking towards the door stopping at the archway.

"By betraying me you have betrayed yourself. Our love was only a portal, Amana. A portal that I have kept open. You wanted it closed long before now. I finally allow your desire." He slowly shut the portal behind him and the dark ice ended with an extended thud.

ZORATH LED a covert team of four with Rascoth and two fully armored generals brandishing heavy *paxes*, tall and wide maiming weapons held with two hands to balance their weight. He mentioned nothing to his twin about his failing, shortly before he had found him talking to one of the generals. They moved swiftly through the large empty corridors of the Battlekeep. Guards, servants and mistresses were absent as if all swooshed away by invisible hands.

The four reached a set of engraved double doors and upon reaching them the two generals took their place at each side while Zorath, silver rod firmly in hand, and Rascoth, wielding his ripping-white rader, entered abruptly. Inside they found King Llinduus, an exquisitely dressed Nivian with sharp facial features and a plump but firm body wearing clothes of silver and white. His braided silver hair matched that of his daughters' and he calmly turned to face his uninvited guests unsurprised by their presence here. Noble white eyes examined the two.

"You are at ends, King," said Zorath, confident that all was in place. "Your end and my beginning."

"Finally, you have arrived." Llinduus paused momentarily choosing to crunch a fresh shard of ice. "My daughter just spoke with me," he said as the shard turned to liquid in his mouth and it washed down into his body. Amana became visible from where she had been standing unseen by the surprised guests. She had been talking plainly to her father. Zorath's orange eyes gave a hard look at his soon-to-be ex-wife.

"She is loyal to me first and foremost, and was most upset at what you did to her." Llinduus crunched another shard but Zorath felt as if a piece of ice had been lodged in his own throat.

He cleared his lump in order to speak. "A double edged shard is your daughter much like her father," Zorath muttered. Rascoth had quietly moved to the background. "It is unfortunate that her seedling was mine."

"That is unfortunate, Zorath," said Amana, cold and shallow. "But you are aware of many things. More than, even I, anticipated."

"And there will be more," replied Zorath.

"You are mistaken and at your end, Commander," said Llinduus downplaying his title in a sneer. "In Nivata, I command."

"Perhaps, but perhaps not," said Zorath and held out the rod pointing it to the King. "This is where I begin."

Unafraid, Llinduus said, "Your greatest error, fatal as it seems, has been your keeping of passion. Control knows no passion, no comfort – only

purpose. But the very purpose in you is
contaminated with passion."

As soon as the white sphere illuminated from the
rod's tip a blue ray flashed out from a wall and
stifled it. Surprise coated Zorath's eyes.

"It makes you weak and unfit to be King of
Nivata," the king continued. "This is why you have
remained in your post for so long."

Llinduus rotated his left hand and a force of
silvery-blue energy, strong enough to decimate any
lesser Nivian, struck Zorath by surprise and sent
him reeling through the closed double doors. He
landed with his entire chest scorched to his ice flesh,
stunned, and the marbled floor shattered beneath
his heavy weight. Llinduus disappeared and flashed
himself next to his enemy's horizontal body, spell
already prepared, and cast out. Zorath was ready
and deflected it into a near wall. Zorath flashed a
safe distance away to center himself. Again
Llinduus was there, this time with a large two-
handed ice paxe, picked up from thin air. Rod and
paxe clashed several fruitless times before a ray of
bright flamma erupted from the white ball at the
end of the long rod and it cut the King's arm off
forcing him to wield the paxe in one hand. The
curved blade ripped into flesh. Zorath repositioned
himself then used the rod's power again, this time
Llinduus partially deflected it with the paxe, it
evaporated, and the sudden flash of flamma
exploded in his hands as a small bursting star. The
King was sent reeling backwards.

Zorath, just before he was to make the final strike, got hit twice from behind by the two paxe-wielding generals. Without compassion or delay he erupted a sufficient radius around him in a brilliant orange that melted all the extremities of his two new enemies, they dropped the paxes and screamed in dire agony without being able to soothe its effects; he turned once again on Llinduus who by now had nearly recovered.

"My passion...is your dissolution." He said calmly before releasing the full power of the rod and only a moment before Llinduus released his own spell. The ray of flamma disintegrated Llinduus and continued to cut a 200 meter section of Kalimantan sending a large piece crashing down the sheer hull. A blizzard of ice, wind, and flamma filled the corridor and masked all inside. All Zorath could see was the haze of his future and all he knew for certain was the arvicity flowing through Seca and into him. When it calmed, Zorath saw Rascoth and Amana side by side but without smiles as should have been. Then he understood more clearly why they did not interfere in the battle just now. He had been played and now all of his flaw was realized. It was their plan for him to kill Llinduus.

Before he could react, Rascoth, already prepared far in advance, threw a spell that made the rod vanish from Zorath's hands and appeared in his hand. Then while he was still stunned at what happened, his twin brother cast another spell that dropped the handsome mirror image to the ground choking in his own naqui. Zorath, half sprawled on the ground and critically injured, stared at the broken floor wondering how he failed and made the most crucial mistake of all. The cracked floor laughed at him. But he already knew his mistake. Llinduus was right. A pair of beautiful legs moved closer defocusing his attention.

"Why Amana?" he asked, still choking and spitting naqui. "Why?"

"You are wrong to think there is a reason. As you told me once before, Zorath, reasons are redundant excuses we fool ourselves to believe. And you still ask me why? If it is something that you must believe then believe that your seedling is not yours."

Zorath choked more trying to speak but still unable. Another hit would certainly claim his life. He was recalling a spell, an escape, but it was unmanageable and had not full formed yet.

"Yes, brother, it seems that many things are not yours and because of you they are mine. It will be my hand that rules, not yours. Kalimantan will be mine! The cosmos will be mine to shape!" Rascoth turned the rod toward the dying Nivian. Zorath clenched his throat. In the time it took to glance, the rader was drawn and Amana's head removed at the chest as the rader ripped through her flesh sending shards of her all over. The chunk of upper body dropped to the floor like a large bluish iceball. Naqui from his slain wife splashed over Zorath's eyes and dripped as blue tears onto the floor.

"My hand, brother!" cried Rascoth.

"Did she tell you...tell you that Llinduus had already made you King?" Zorath said, thinking quickly and not aware of what had really happened to the love of his life. He was still faced down hoping it would have the effect he desired. It did.

Rascoth lowered the rod and rader, then he turned to look at Amana's body. And in the space of that look was all that he needed to get up and jump off of the ledge he had previously cut, not before taking the rod from his brother's relaxed hand after he struck him in the eyes with the edge of a broken tile of the flooring. In mid-flight he managed with difficulty to cast his long prepared spell to exit planum Nivata and disappeared on his descent.

"Zorath! Zorath!" yelled Rascoth as he ran up to the ledge washing the naqui from his sight and in time to see his brother vanish into cold air. Llinduus' physical trace filled the air he breathed. No one remained.

Rascoth stared at the empty air far down below. The wind howled, taunting him, reminding him. His hair blew wildly. And with his back towards the edge he rotated his head to where his twin brother jumped off thinking to himself, "Goodbye, brother. Here we part."

Zorath could visualize falling a great distance through an open gateway and then appearing in an ice storm. He thought that his spell had failed to take him from Nivata and cursed his actions. In his blinded and dying state he cast a protection spell from his amulet just as he crashed through a sheet of packed ice and drowned in a shake of consuming frost and wind.

Chapter 2

SOFT SPOKEN and carefully chosen verse exited from the mouth of the entan Tulai Khan as he verbalized his extensive knowledge of reanimation and transcribed it onto his unbound manuscript.

"Grab some *palp* for your ageing father, Calil," Tulai said to his first seedling by the right of his chair. "Your father's eyes grow weary and his thoughts approach resolution."

"Palp," Calil, a luto seedling of 180 tios, had already begun moving to retrieve a new stack of *palpfere*, palp as it was called by most, made of a thin sheet of translucent cora, for his father to inscribe on.

Tulai, without looking, took the fresh stack of cora-pressed fibrous sheets and immediately placed them under the *inscriptor*, a flamma-based ceramic lamp designed to translate sound into visual script. His own invention.

Tulai Khan was an inventor. He was a creator of things. His most recent work was about the reconnection of life and death and had kept him occupied for more time than he could remember. His partner and wife Lez-win had grown accustomed to his quirky yet brilliant cerbus, brain, and didn't seem to be bothered to tend to the house and their two young seedlings, Calil and Shev'la, though the second had grown sick and weak from coriatic disease, an abnormal condition that weakened the entan corius affecting the circulation of milk and energy.

He had discovered by stringent *cosmiscience*, formerly known as cosmic science until his incredible revelations were realized – previously unfound in the teachings of Seranor – that the *kol* the life factor and essence of all beings, could be rejoined with the body given sufficient time to recollect it and bring it back. He was proud of his reanimation theory, yet calm at the same time.

The past thirty days had kept him completely occupied with finishing the first draft of his manuscript titled *The Anativical Theorem I*, with unsolved parts lingering inside without an apparent answer destined to wait for the right moment when all would come together by way of some innocuous catalyst. Tulai remained a young luto full of passion uncommon in local Seronians; despite deep investments of cerbal energy and manipulating *arvicity*, energy fields permeating the planet, along with his lengthened age.

The thirtieth day after the start of the reanimation manuscript, Tulai had remained working throughout the night to produce more palp to finish burning the *elos* (elliptical language of Seranor) glyphs. He worked quietly and calmly as though he had imbibed a youth potion; he whispered sounds into the inscriptor and slowly rotated the palpfere so that a circular placement of elos found its way around the entire sheet of fibers; then he suddenly stopped, sat back on the seat, and turned to the smallish and curious seedling beside him.

The brimming smile of his white porcelan face was instantly noticed. He swung his long silvery hair back proud of his accomplishment and his over-sized rounded eyes gleamed in completion. Other entans, inhabitants of Seranor, envied his youthful looks and if not for his strangely colored hair he could pass for not much more than his seedling's age. Tulai's most prominent feature, disregarding his lanky body, was his slightly bulging eyes, a rare semi-circle of gray and one of green together, that emanated a luminescent vitality.

There was a moment of silence filled with the knowledge of completion. It was done.

"Father, is it really completed?" Calil asked in an excited voice.

There was a pause before Tulai finally spoke. "Completed. It is done..." He picked up the inch-thick manuscript and held it above Calil's head with his right hand.

Calil tilted his head up so he could see it. He smiled, happy to see his father complete the theory that might one day keep Seronians alive forever, as they had once been born. But there was something else behind the silence of his father that caused Calil's smile to wither for that finer moment. It was a question of whether the right door had been opened and what corridor had been carved.

"It is done Calil. Let us go outside and enjoy Nata for a moment. Her winds will carry our thoughts into a more pleasant place," he said in a reassuring voice, knowing that he had entered through a barrier which had no discernable outcome, and pushing Calil harder and harder with his left hand.

"I'm going father," he replied feeling somewhat uneasy about being pushed out the portal.

"I guess your father is tired and has lost his control of strength," the exhausted Tulai started suddenly seeing how his poor mood had shifted onto his seedling. "Sorry, Calil…Come and let us go outside where the wind will give us new vigor. To clear our cerbinds of what we have done."

EVEN CALIL understood that his father had reached a point beyond where most would not ever dare. All Seronians were gifted with the greatest intellects and abilities save a handful that were deemed less than perfect. Where most wallowed in those gifts others like Tulai challenged his intellect and pushed the skin of life further than most others dreamed of. Calil looked at him with bright proud eyes. What Tulai saw in his eyes was love, but what he could not know was the responsibility that he had brought upon himself.

Just then the front portal opened, probably Lezwin thinking ahead as she always did, and a short draft came from under the door into the room. The fresh air revived Tulai's kol and he opened the door to the hall hugging Calil and gently rocking to and fro as they floated together out the door. As they passed the door his wife was waiting with *qualls*, fist-sized spheres of semi-frozen and flavored aqua, and they enjoyed the glowing night over Seranor's landscape.

"Nata brings her greetings again this day," Lezwin said and her long hair flowed unpredictably in the wind. "Calil, can you find your brother and see what he has been doing."

"But I want to stay with father and talk about—"

"Go and find Shev'la! I just don't want him to wander alone again. He has been getting more and more distant as of late," she wouldn't let him finish and turned her face sternly to him as a mother would. Calil looked at his father for support but he was staring out into the cloud-filled blue sky. Without any response Calil had no choice but to go after his younger brother.

"I asked you before not to complete this project. Why do you refuse to accept what it is I have asked?" she said.

"After discovering Anativo everything has changed. It is like a new door has been opened for me and this new path led me to see what was once invisible to my cerbind," he spoke with an excitement as a child who had found a new toy. "There is noxy in my milk and it burns me in the cold, penetrating forests. I have found the answer! I have—"

"There is a reason that it hasn't yet been discovered. Maybe it wasn't meant to," she waited until Calil had gone some distance and then turned her head towards Tulai who returned his stare into the blue clouds, a permanent blanket shielding Seranor.

"It's done. It's done. I had to do it. I could no longer sleep at night nor work nor consider anything. I was a Seraniva's serf for I had lost my own thoughts," he said without turning his head to his wife. "If not I, then who?"

"Then someone else would find it and be given its responsibility and not you," she blurted out, getting more excited by the word. "None of us know what you have done. Anativo is not a toy, he is more powerful than the Malkar...He stands for everything that can deconstruct the entan world...Now even Calil has interest in this. And you haven't seen Shev'la for more than a month. You *forgot* your sick seedling!" She pronounced the word forgot and felt loss and separation.

HE FACED her, and the expression of anger on her face made him feel remorse. He could not fully understand what had caused her to become so hurt at such a great accomplishment in the history of Seranor. No, he thought, she cannot do this to me; I have found the secret to keeping all Seronians alive forever by breaking the key between Seranor's life and our lives. "I have saved Seronians – saved them all!" he shouted.

At that moment the cry of two seedlings, in the short distance around the corner of the house, alerted the both of them; they ran over to find Shev'la lying on the ground and Calil crying over his motionless body.

"Father, why does he collapse so?" said the younger seedling while crying over his unconscious step brother. Calil was born of Calillian, Tulai's first wife who died an unexplained death several decades after his birth.

"It is his corius which does not serve him well. You must look after your brother," Tulai said trying to restore confidence.

"Yes, father."

Tulai motioned his hands over Shev'la's still and gray-skinned body. The pool of arvicity flowed and circled until it ran through his hands. The hands changed motion, collected the arvic waves and reshaped them before sending them out into a soft white hue over his seedling. The gray once again turned to white porcelan skin and Shev'la's silvery blue eyes opened; he looked straight then to both sides before realizing that he was on the ground.

"Rise up, for your mother worries about you," his father knelt down on his right knee and helped him to sit up.

"Mother? Where is mother?" he asked with a feint voice.

"Behind you," she held red tears in her eyes and wiped them roughly before Shev'la would worry. "Give your mother a hug so that she may know that you have returned to her." He rose and, with a slight wobble, walked over to his mother. Tulai, facing his seedling's back, looked into Lez-win's eyes and gave a look that said that this was nearing the last time that they could do this to him. His corius had been deteriorating since his birth 150 tios ago.

Tulai had so focused on his own work that he had neglected his second seedling and now that look from his wife, mother to Shev'la, made him feel all those tios of neglect put together – guilt for one's first responsibilities. Lez-win picked up Shev'la, straddled his legs around her curvy figure, and started off for their *unamid*, a singular tall-standing residence created and owned by them.

Lez-win pressed her mouth together and stood directly beside her husband so that he could hear her words.

"Saved all of Seranor, have you?" she said briefly turning her head towards her absentminded husband. "Saved all Seronians except the ones closest to you." The sarcasm resonated with feelings of true disappointment as she walked off. Tulai wanted to speak but decided that she was right.

"Go with your mother, Calil," he said while he patted him on the left shoulder.

SHEV'LA NOW slept peacefully in the upstairs cell. Tulai Khan stayed outside feeling the windy breeze on his face. The wind flowed softly over his smooth white porcelan skin and soothed him. "Nata," he said to himself. "Why do you always hide and only comfort us when it pleases you? Are you still angry with me?" There was no answer.

Nata, the wind spirit of Seranor whose unpredictable nature and force came and went as she pleased, was listening. "I know why you do not answer me, Nata," Tulai replied to himself. "It is because you are neither here nor there. The wisest of us all. You are the unknown secret to our planet for without you the balance would be forgotten. And so you hide but are not lost though often unrecognized. Sometimes I wish I could be like this but I am just an entan and nothing more." This fact disappointed him. A gust of wind slapped his face. "My seed dies and I have forgotten him in my hunger to be more than myself. I have pushed my limits from my past and my Shev'la is in pain."

His head was down watching the cora grass move to and fro in the wind's caress. No, he's going to die! He is going to die. And what is most horrible about his death is that it is my failing that will kill him. I will have killed him yet I had nothing to do with it. If he died then I would have not only killed Calillian but also my second seedling, he thought. "This cannot happen. Cannot. Must not happen," he muttered in fervor to himself stressing the words *must not* as if trying to motivate himself to prevent imminent death.

He remembered once again his theories on reanimation and how they joined a separated kol and body but what happened to the sick and those in the process of dying? he questioned to himself. Calillian's face appeared in his head. His seedling Shev'la had been born at a time of deep involvement in reanimation experimentation. He had consumed his arvic energy while finalizing the rebirth spells. Nata was forced to help. Maybe it was his exhausted energy that had been transferred to his seedling as a constant reminder to his failings as a father. A reminder to his dedication to being a genius.

He could no longer accept death as an option for another death in his family would surely forever reverberate into tomorrow. He could not deceive the truer need of his own ambitions as a luto gifted with the power of creation, superior intelligence, young corius, needed by Seranor and Seronians, of which he was one. He could not deny his love for his wife Lez-win, a pure white-skinned luta with glossy red eyes and long white hair who was both lover to him and mother to his family. He tried to forgive himself for not paying attention sooner to the seriousness of the illness and the ramblings of his wife. She reminded him time after time but the draw of his own corrupt vision was blinded by his need to be recognized amongst the *ceramin* before he grew too old to be able to taste the flavor of respect and admiration. He had never considered it carefully as to what the effects might be to dedicate to one task so fervently and to others so casually, but had probably known from the start that the pain of his own seedling pushed him away in fear of failing to save his life before finishing the one true thing that could keep all alive forever.

Mistakes could be made. Tulai said to himself. Just as long as solutions are made to suit them. And solutions will come indeed. I will solve my seedling's illness and take back what I gave of myself. It was a mistake! There was something irregular about sacrificing your seedling for true knowledge. It was in the power of knowledge that I have been blinded. Even if this knowledge could save all Seronians and beings on planet Seranor, I should have never allowed myself to forget those that mattered the most to my life for it was the cause of my pain now. Saving one hundred does not take precedence over saving the one. It was a choice and not a requirement. I chose to save the hundred, but given the choice again I would choose anew, which is to protect any life – the plural comes from the singular.

Time for a solution, Tulai said to himself; he lifted up his head, adjusted his fallen pants, breathed in deeply, threw back his hair, went to the back of the unamid with his purposeful step; waved his hand at the unseen doorway and stepped quickly inside the darkened hall to his chamber of experiments.

THE CHAMBER hallway led to a circular cell some 30 meters in any direction. Clean, sterile and well organized. Equipment, technological devices, processing materials, liquids, aqua and various potions fitted into the furnishings around the cell. Most were white lutium-based devices with command glyphs on them. They were of various sizes and shapes and organized neatly along the shelves or on the tables, with all of them made of a simple but refined design. An area was reserved for all palp-based materials, some was locked out of sight and others were stored on shelves designed to carry palpfere manuscripts neatly. At the center of the cell was an empty spot with a circular ring signifying the Torq of Seranor, two intertwined giant serpents contained in a ring. It had been modified slightly and detailed to show the deeper relationships between the legendary and natural forces of Seranor and Seragorn.

Large flamma patches glowed from the ceiling and cast natural light in the cell while some areas remained strangely darker than others. To the far side was a lit area with a long resting table structure made of white lutium. A tall blue-skinned figure, some two and a half meters in length, encased in a block of blue lay there quietly. There was a black device radiating sub-zero temperatures around it. A hole had been burned into the large object and a long syringe-like device with a soft ceramic pipe connected the blue being with the black lutium contraption on the table beside it.

Three translucent globes rested on both sides of this device. The left globe contained a coarse blue mixture while the right was semi-filled with a white liquid similar in composition to milk, the white blood of all entans.

"It is you I must both thank and blame Anativo for my current circumstance," Tulai said to himself while walking up to the encased being. He named him Anativo because of his relationship to the Anativical Theorem. "If not for your icy blue naqui milk, I may have spent many decades trying to solve our fates. Now we must save my seedling and you will help me once again. In return I promise to bring you back from your state and we shall all share in the glory of tomorrow and hope that your chance being here this day will not be a moment of regret, rather the template for the future."

Chapter 3

HE RETURNED to the center of the Seronian Torq inset onto the ceramic inlaid floor, cast out both arms to his side and began mumbling the twisted verse of Arvicians known as ogun. The verse enabled Arvicians to manipulate the arvic oceans that flow in and around the planet. The energies of Seranor and Seragorn, her seed, had been connected during their enslavement and now all practitioners and manipulators of arvicity shared the same oceans of energized pools. Users of Seranor's energy cast spells of white and brilliance under the banner of opus, the planet's true and balanced power that allowed creation to begin in the days of origin. Seragorn, angered by those that murdered his mother, breathed energy in bursts and whose oceans were torrid and violent. Blue-hued arvic spells glowed from those that followed ora and its new power. Deep followers of ora turned to using arvicity for purely destructive purposes and became Arvicerers, gray skinned lute bent on dividing the land and claiming it for themselves.

Tulai was never even a good generalist Arvician but he had mastered arvicity to control and manipulate the life of beings. It had been 40 tios since anyone called him an Arvician; instead, he was known as a *Nexitist*, one who was consumed with the nexa, death of the body, and joined kol and body after they had been separated.

Nexitix was a lonely art that Tulai didn't really choose yet it found its way into his life and after having touched his ability had led him down a long path where others dared not follow. He never considered ideas carefully or new information; ideas rather came to him in times of calmness and openness, just as he picked the clothes he would wear that day. As he lived in a small society gifted with intelligence and ability, such as all areas on planet Seranor, it was important if not to the point of imperative that he remained different to the crowd in fear of being forgotten in the days yet to come. He, like many, did enjoy the times of the peaceful life and occasionally sought out others to spend time with, but Tulai was born of a curious

nature bent on exploring what hadn't been explored
and solving problems that others could not or cared
not about. This curious nature about him led him to
search for the connection of life on Seranor to her
spirit. More than that, it was the death of his first
wife, Calillian, that indeed provoked him to delve
into an area seen as the space between opus and ora
for it was in nexa, death, that life was renewed. He
could not accept, as others easily did, the death of
one whom he loved more than he loved himself, and
after losing that, his love turned inward and became
a focused consumption of all that he was and
believed.

He created things, of which few knew were from
his original ideas, like palpfere used to inscribe the
elos script which was developed from his elos verse;
an elliptical and highly visual verse suited to the
high intellects of Seronians. Palp, as it was called,
was used to transcribe knowledge so that it could be
transferred to others and further developed to
increase the knowledge level of all society.
Manuscripts were written on palp and many hidden
in fear of the getting lost in the hands of the karul or
cerbors or even lost to ventans, the grayed entans.
He had even heard of one arvatist who in the
southern *urba* Casus had created a regular feature
of information and called it a *palpazine* though not
many were interested in this new type of
communication medium.

If there was any reason why he preferred the
dead to the living, which nearly all chose though
some chose to extinguish life also, it was not because

he thought it more important but because it suited the quiet life he began to lead after Calillian. Death to him brought him a new life and having once tasted true death first hand, he so clung to it as his savior and familiar partner to guide him to the next life. Death was made a certainty and life an unpredictability.

The life of all lute was sure to expire in 1,200 tios. Even the eldest only lived to 1,500 tios. Death, it was said, was already scheduled for us all, just the departure was different. Two kinds of departure prevailed on the planet. The first was the most basic and most prevalent as nearly all entans would soon enough be turned into ceramic dust and then cast out upon the land after one month of time had elapsed. Ceramification was the second form of departure though this was reserved for the most accomplished. Some were given a choice at the time of their birth. Most were not. The ancient heroes of the land remained in petrified porcelan. Statues, they were called by Seronians. Every town or urba had a hall of statues so that those who had left their influence could be remembered. More prominent statues were put in front of buildings and in the ceramin's squares. Tulai's first wife, Calillian, remained a statue. It pained Tulai to see her. Her statue was moved into Ceramin Square and was the reason why he refused to hold any lectures in Ulaq. He could not bear to see her for it reminded him of what he had failed to do.

Tulai didn't buy into the common way of thinking about death, and could not understand the detraction to one aspect of nature, cosmic reality about what all beings will feel when living was composed by nature to have these two aspects. Life, seen as unpredictable and challenging, was held by the fact that life could not be scheduled, and yet that was further from the truth, since all Seronians were gifted with the fate of all things and how their interaction with it would be.

On the same hand that Tulai studied death, he also enjoyed to create communication devices, not for speaking to the dead, rather for decreasing the communicative distance that was currently limiting society. He recently developed a coded messaging system so that others may not understand the message unless they could break the code. Strangely enough it was Shev'la who took interest in his discarded work on codes and preferred breaking codes rather than making them.

Tulai supported the introduction and use of technological gadgetry designed to supplement life even though many feared that technology may yet one day cause a great revolution against nature. He found it convenient to order non-food items necessary for living using the *flashpods*, circular ceramic rings embedded with arvic glyphs. Shoppers would go to a central area in the town or urba and select the non-food items. These would then be flashed over to the appropriate cell such as a unamid. Researchers had been working on flashing clay food but organic compounds still had many failings. The clay would often come through overcooked or would simply vanish through disintegration.

After finishing his arvic exercises and verse, he adjusted himself and his clothes, reached back his arms and stared briefly at Anativo. He smiled, not because of his fortune – the optimistic smile was a result of hope for Shev'la's future. Tulai poured out the remainder of the strange colored naqui into a white porcelan flask.

A seed's voice became louder from outside; Tulai recognized it as Calil.

Why is he up so late? thought Tulai, his mother should have put him to bed hours ago. He went through the entrance to meet him. Calil ran up to his father to greet him, embraced him as he hadn't seen him for a long time and when he backed off Tulai wouldn't let him go.

"Why are you still up?" he asked then realized that it was bright outside and that Calil had already had his daily morning bath leaving his white skin and black hair smooth and shiny. He was aware that Shev'la wasn't there, and tried to accept his reasons knowing full well his role in their relationship.

"It's morning. Mother asked me to find you," Calil answered.

"Yes, father has been working all through the dark," he said trying to justify where he'd been for so long then he remembered the flask in his hand. "Look Calil, I've made something special for your brother."

"What is it?"

"It will heal your brother's weak system," he added some excitement to this response which enlivened Calil.

Calil knew about Shev'la's sickness and his father's neglect, that his mother had pestered his father since Shev'la was born, that his father was too preoccupied to listen intently, and that now it was all maybe too late, his belated efforts trying to fix things. Calil ignored it as he had often done since he also knew that his brother was nearing his death bed and his father was unaware of how far the weakness had advanced. Tulai, this time, was bent on changing what he had done before.

They walked briskly together to inside the family cell where his wife had prepared some warm clay for the morning feast. Lez-win was cooking attentively as if bent on taking her cerbind off of her other more disturbing thoughts. Tulai saw this and knew that his role today would be that of the problem solver.

"Lez, I've created something new this morning..."

"New! Oh well let us celebrate again. What is it this day? You found the Nivian's brother and he's going to stay for dinner tonight!" sarcasm oozed out of her mouth and she was more than anything letting off steam.

"No. Something better. Something for Shev'la," he said not bothered by her wild remark.

"Is that going to help Shev'la, father?" asked Calil.

"Help it will," he answered and motioned to stroke the back of his Calil's neck. "It is a special potion to rejuvenate his milk, Lez. Once it gets enough

energy, the milk will have the properties to heal
itself and restore its strength to maximum capacity,"
he said trying to avoid the scientific terminology but
wanting to explain so they could better understand.

"Potions! Isn't it a little late for potions? Your
seed is dying, Tulai! Dying!" she said getting more
and more excited as she spoke. "No potion will save
him now. He is so weak that he can't even come to
eat."

"But this is the solution, Lez. And it is because of
our Nivian friend that we have this," Tulai tried to
justify what he did realizing that it was a mistake on
his part that it waited so long.

"Nivians don't make friends, Tulai. Have you
thought of that?" she said.

"Of course I have, but once I reanimate him he
will be very thankful and will be open to friendship,"
he said but knew that Nivians were the rulers of
Nivata, of ora, and that they only knew ruling and
knew not how to be ruled nor friendship especially
with their enemies. Nivians were the greatest
Arvicerers. Some of them had the potential to
manipulate all of Seragorn's arvicity and to strike
down the only blockade to their achieving their
ultimate goal. But there was more than just reason
for Anativo being found in Nivata Lake.

"You've thought of everything then," she quickly
replied. "Now let's eat."

"Where's Shev'la?"

"He's too sick to come here. I will bring him some
food," she said.

"I will go," Tulai said trying to increase his involvement with his dying seed. He turned and headed towards the upstairs cell.

What will he think of me? he thought. An inner voice said to him that he must save him, that should he die so too will Seranor die and all of his own hopes shall soon be dead because there was some immeasurable connection between his seedling and the future. Something must begin to change now even if it is the smallest change; and change was in Tulai's nature. Things will be changed and one change will cause another until all things had been satisfied. "We start now," he said.

Chapter 4

SHEV'LA, HIS once shiny silver-blue eyes now a dull gray and half-closed with his brittle silver hair hiding the emptiness inside, was sitting on the bed only wearing his favorite cora silk pajamas his mother tailored for him on his fiftieth birth tios celebration. The room was full of strange flammic devices that somewhat resembled his father's failed communicative creations and had been renovated by spare effort alone.

When he heard his father's voice he moved from the contemplative sitting position, looking at the portal and made a futile attempt to put on an air of confidence. He felt that his father had abandoned him for more important projects in life, and was unsure what to say or discuss should they meet face to face. He was only trying to stay alive, to recuperate enough before another coriatic failure would stand still his life for an eternal moment. It had been more than a hand and a half of questionable moments when his loss of consciousness once again opened the sky and he was made to climb the glowing flammic ladder, nexa, that ended in utter brilliance.

Seronians called it the *scala of immortality* for it was known that those who climbed the ladder could become divine with the knowledge and power over all things. Many Seronians found both pleasure and power in drinking the mixture called *anascal* which enlightened them to the portal, the realm of Seranivas, speakers of secrets of arvicity and life using twisted of verse. Shev'la knew that his time was near and his ascension was made more certain as the days passed, but hated his fate as much as he hated his father now.

At only 150 tios he felt that his dreams were yet unfulfilled, and his nightmares were put in their place, it was pure hurt to see his father to achieve only to take away from him. His physical misdirection and ailing intellect allowed him to occupy his creative quotient pushing his cerbus into its limit. He derived that he could no longer escape his nexa, but, delaying the inevitable, he kept creating devices of communication and imagining a life undecided. If he could only crack the unseen code to his pathetic condition he could be made free from the bindings of disease. That on his climb to divinity he would garner favoritism for his minor accomplishments as a seedling.

When his father did knock on the ceramic portal, he pretended not to listen, pretending to be completely focused on the odd shaped communication device in his hand, and soon enough called the gutra sound to release the portal's position. But his face remained on his current task with the forced look of determination, though pain and fear were more difficult to disguise.

"Shev'la!" his father said in a sharp, energetic tone. He lifted his chest and tried to look as if tomorrow will not compare to the woes of today, while radiating guilt nonetheless. "Shev'la, I have found the cure to your illness. See here in my hand."

Shev'la hesitated then could not resist the slow turn of his head and staring at his father's boots and moving up to the hands all the while trying to avoid looking directly at his face. Wow, he thought, he's found a cure just as my life is finished. I'm glad that he remembered...It's that optimistic nature in him, which everyone believes for one reason or another; that optimism he carries – I don't want it! he decided. He blinked slowly and sighed.

"It's too late!" he said trying to sound angry but coming out condescending.

"Shev'la!" he said once more, his voice running faster and faster. "I haven't forgotten you...just for little while...but now I have truly discovered the most powerful potion ever made for an entan."

"It won't work. Nothing will work anymore," he mumbled.

"It will. It is—"

"I don't want it, I don't want it, I don't want it!" he cried out turning his head quickly away from his father, as though the cry was a plea for help.

Tulai hadn't been concerned about his second seed, he thought that the deterioration in his health would "level off," as his *cosmiscience*-based friends often put it, and managed to stay directed with his own preoccupations. But to see his brittle face resigned to hopelessness and waiting for resolution, he found it difficult to breathe, and his eyes grew dark red.

"Who have I forgotten! Shev'la! I have been—" He lost his breath and could no longer continue.

Shev'la dropped the device in his hands and stared up at his father.

"Please—what can we do now? Listen to your father one last time…trust me…I am still your father who cared for you for all your tios except the last one…only the last one…no, no, not the last one…" He realized that his very words had sanctioned Shev'la's end and knelt down while reaching out his left hand.

Shev'la tried to avoid his touch but lacked the strength to move as any normal entan could. He looked down and became further hopeless, if that were possible on the last limbs of life, all the while waiting for his father to give a reason to continue.

"I have saved all Seronians..." he blurted out wanting to continue but Shev'la collapsed further towards the warm ceramic tiles.

"I want not your help father! Not want anything from you!" he yelled out in a guttural voice, "and say not another phrase of your newest inventions!"

He clamored to get up, staggered twice before repositioning himself so that he could carry his weight. Tulai tried to grab his son to hug him as he so desperately wanted to but as he reached out Shev'la moved out his way only to lose his balance, his father caught his fall before crashing though his left arm hit the wall on his way up and cracked as milk came out.

"Shev'la!' he said, by now breathing heavily in worry. "Please, think of your mother, she cares so much for you, it's not her fault. It is me who has forgotten; hate me, but give me a chance to save you for your mother's sake. I have the solution at hand! I have failed with you, I don't want to fail your mother! I have failed until this time. Now, trust me once more and I will not fail again!"

Shev'la relaxed. His father could feel the struggle diminishing, and he felt completely responsible for him. Shev'la tried to speak a number of times, but the energy failed him. His father remained quiet.

"You see mother as the light in your darkened world, but I see her as the one who has suffered," said his dying seed. "I love my mother and would not want to cause her any more pain, but I am uncertain about how I can – by my nexa, or your blinded self imprisonment – yes, imprisonment...My skin is failing, my milk is failing, after today – after I am gone, will you show your true kindness to my mother? Is it in you to do such a thing? Tell me—"

"Your hopelessness is my hope. Your fear is my strength and you will not be gone – will not!" He said in a confident voice knowing full well what he was saying, and hugging his seed closer and closer. "I remember what was said to me on the day of your birth, you will be the photon in Seranor's delusion. You will be the catalyst of the serpent's revenge."

"Your words are just – sounds! You do not know how to help me. You're afraid and it is why you hide in your chamber cell – yes, afraid!"

Tulai looked at him, the feelings of fear and anger on his weakened face. It was a reflection of his own fears that he saw in his seed's eyes. Shev'la collapsed in his arms. Just then Lez-win, who had probably been listening the whole time, entered the cell with red tears streaming down her soft white cheeks.

"Have I been so bad, Lez?" he turned to his wife speaking with muttered words, briefly looking up but not waiting for the answer he already knew. She remained silent at first.

"Can you really help, Tulai? Our seed will die if he is not saved. You said you can save all Seronians, what about your own essence? What good is all of Seranor without those that you love the most?" She silently walked away and returned downstairs.

"Father," mumbled Shev'la with his face in his father's cora clothing, "have you neglected your family so that you may become a statue?"

"No, Shev'la. I have not considered such a thing. I would not trade you nor mother nor Calil for such a thing. I do not care if I am dust."

The weak seed lifted his head. "Father, will I become a statue?"

"If that is what you want then it is possible."

"Polinatum has said that only those who achieve the highest level of...realization...can choose to be petrified in porcelan. Can I choose it?"

"Is that what you want, my seed?"

"What I want, father? I am dying, father. As I die I would like to know if I will be made a statue so that all may remember me."

"You are not dead, Shev'la. Choosing ceramification will come much later in your life. Do not count your death until all of the flamma is extinguished. Is all the flamma extinguished?"

"No, father."

"Then you are not dead."

"It is dark and cold..." With that, Shev'la faded into a sleep. Tulai threw a spell to comfort him in his sickness.

I can and I will save him, he said to himself, recalling Shev'la's cries and pain. This task I will do and make him stronger than any Seronian. Tulai stood up, still holding his seed, raised his head, breathed out and in once in full, and went out of the unamid.

Chapter 5

TULAI'S ABILITY as an Arvician proved its worth once
more as he extracted Anativo's naqui, mixed then
transfused it into his seed's degenerated body.
Augmented and unnatural regeneration rolled
through Shev'la's very atomic structure as nights
churned through days churning once more into the
months. Hollowness was replaced by density,
lifelessness by vibrancy, weakness by energy.
Shev'la's body refashioned itself anew. Stronger and
stronger Tulai's seed became until, after 10 tios, the
dullness of Shev'la's eyes had brightened as if a noxy
fire reflected in the lenses of his eyes. His kol

hummed and his porcelan skin became supple and strong against the hardest of blows, and a new character emerged.

Seedhood friends in the town soon grew jealous as Shev'la gained in not only health but speed and strength as well. They would talk about him behind his back and having nothing left to say would always revert back to the story of the blue-skinned alien hidden at the back of their residence. Other Seronians, comiscientific partners and colleagues questioned Tulai's responsibilities to Seranor herself and suggested that he had lost his way, been hardened by his own in-depth research in Nexitix.

His closest friend Polinatum, a great Sagmal and counsel to many spread across the lands, also saw the changes in Shev'la and tried to warn Tulai of his actions into areas which no longer were his to judge. This Sagmal was a tall entan, taller than Tulai by a few centimeters, enchanted with high knowledge of Seranor and her seed. Polinatum often made anascal and was reputed to have some of the best brews in the region though he only shared it with his closest colleagues. Confidence and superiority were his flaws and they were often disguised in the form of knowledge used to influence the others. But his most skillful complement was that of emotion and appeal, powerful enough to change most entan cerbi except the most stupid and stubborn.

"Tulai, you simply must surrender this quest that you are on," Polinatum started with an air of desperation. "Many of us feel that the Nivian should have been left for others to find or killed so that none would find him."

"Killed? Is there just not reason for what things may come or is life simply without a path? No—say not what you think for I know that what comes our way did not just come, we also came on its way," Tulai said strongly trying to make the point and to shift the blame from him.

"Talking of ways is not our way, Tulai. Drop this madness or it will madden you!" he answered angrily to his friend's response. For he thought blame always laid in the hands of those who chose rather than the chosen. Life was a series of calculated choices that when made and confirmed by the cosmos opened invisible portals with signs of attraction. His face grew sterner and he took one deep breath in. "You alone have chosen this fate but it shall offend us all if your predictions are wrong."

"He is Nivian and he would not be trapped and dying if he were like the others of Nivata. Something is different about him, albeit I do not know what it is, and I sense that he can help us. Help Seranor. For those of Nivata are like the Kozotal to our society, gifted with abilities that we have not been shown. Yes, there is reason for his being here and my finding him buried in the lake, and he has already influenced our society for the better..."

"Imagine what influence he will have when he is at full," Polinatum started, his face now ever more stern with a deepening sound coming from his voice.

"What will you do when his full influence is felt on Seranor and we are powerless to stop him?"

"You or I cannot be certain of what will happen with him as with ourselves," Tulai said trying to bury the fact that Polinatum was right to be afraid. "We are all at Seranor's fate as she is with ours. It is possible to conceive the notion that she called him here for reasons yet unknown."

"Inconceivable!" Disgusted to hear such barbaric thoughts from a previously intelligent luto, Polinatum turned abruptly and headed out the portal. He stopped just outside the archway. "You have caused this and you will hold the responsibility," he said as a verdict read to the one accused.

Tulai thought to himself, without Anativo I could not have accomplished so much nor saved my dying seedling so how can he say such things about me. How can he? He—he who is full of arrogance. I will not listen this occasion. Now it is time to bring our savior to full life and then we may all share in our discoveries. Then they will know what I have done is for the good of all and this will extinguish their fear of things that they cannot so readily understand.

Shev'la came out of the chamber just then as Polinatum was walking away in definite strides.

"Is everything all right, father?" Shev'la asked after watching the image in the background walking away. He had grown strong and radiant over the term of his recuperation. His speed and reflex surpassed those of his colleagues and even his father. Shev'la grew not only in physicality but also grew deep levels of intelligence as if the cerbi were exponentially shifting upon itself and completely reforming what it had once formed until the new outmatched the old. This was then repeated time and time again. His arvic weight (AW), the ability of cerbus and body to resonate arvicity, had changed and attained a special numerical value. The value had changed numerous times over his regeneration process, until it finally rested on its current state shortly after the transfusions were stopped.

"All right," he answered calmly but roughly as if restrained by his emotions.

"I've finished preparing the device but—"

"I will do it. Come, let's make history," he said while shuffling his healthy seed by the shoulder. "Tomorrow will be a blue day."

IT WAS late in the day when Tulai and his two seeds Calil and Shev'la entered the chamber of arvic manipulation. His wife, not condoning such behavior in the first place, remained out in the town square with friends and colleagues discussing matters more suited to her requisite tastes. She had fought in the morning in a vain attempt to stop this insanity especially after Polinatum explained to her the importance and potential trouble that could be caused should Anativo arise on Seranor.

It had been 10,000 tios since any Nivian had walked the land belonging to Seranor loathe to remember what damage they had caused to her womb. The last of the Kozotal, not the renegades who stole the Arvinstrum and hid all pieces in the land, but the last of those dedicated to protecting Seranor for her loss would reverberate into the Versos and into the cosmos. The Seranivas learned the secret of Seragorn and taught the Cerbors to steal the Arvinstrum which was used to seal the fates of both mother and seedling. Seragorn's black anger for what they had done still flowed across arvic oceans today.

Nivata, kingdom to all Nivians, was the eternal place of structure and control. It was the antithesis to planet Flamma and of all Kozotal who were the creators of the Versos. Nivians wanted to control planet Aquanomicus; the center of Versos thirty-nine and home to Seranor and Seragorn, the shapers of the planet, to control it, usurp its power and then usurp the energy of the Versos until all things became structured and permanent. Until all things became lifeless as the Realm of Nigratuum'inus where nothing could or would ever exist. It was in the nature of all Nivians to know only this action. An action to control, create structure and impose complete permanence on all things wonderful and beautiful.

Hours had passed since beginning to unthaw Anativo. How he had reached that point no one was sure, many were sure that he shouldn't have been taken from there. It was a cold and windy morning while walking down the snowy path that the threesome decided to stop by the ice lake for a rest.

Calil closed his eyes for some time trying to catch up on lost sleep during the hike before. His father, Tulai, chose to climb a nearby hill to manipulate arvicity and drank some anascal to connect with the Seranivas again. While the two were busy doing their thing, Shev'la, without thought, went playing on the lake. He skated proficiently back and forth across the smooth translucent ice, sometimes on his abdomen and other times on his feet. Jumping and aerial acrobatics were his favorite pastimes ever since he was small so he indulged in his dance-like motions. His body though weak was relatively supple and maneuvered easily in the air without yet the ability to make precision his firm goal.

It was the crack of crystallized aqua, probably of something falling in rather than coming out, that alerted first Tulai then Calil. Shev'la had climbed a tall hill joining the lake and jumped off like an avian would. He had fallen through a thinner part of ice after crashing down hard and landing heavily on one foot. At the time, Tulai was in connection with a Seraniva who had been playing with words of discovery and recovery, of pain and sorrow, and the birth of tomorrow. Tulai was just in the process of finding out more when the loud crack brought him out of his meditative and drunken state. He waved his hands, sounded a word, and off he flew over Calil and directly to a safe area by the hole.

"Shev'la, can you hear me?" his father cried. "Shev'la!"

No response was heard as his seedling had become fully immersed by now and had flowed somewhat away from the hole that brought him in. His cora clothes kept him warm for now but were quickly losing their heating abilities. Cora was known to keep a luto warm or cool for indefinite periods, as long as the cora didn't reach its natural degradation point. But few traveled in icy aqua with only cora to keep them warm and now without the ability to cast a spell to keep him warm frustrated Tulai further.

He couldn't wait any longer so he grabbed a palm-sized circular lutium device with his right arm, spoke a word and looked into it trying to trace Shev'la's arvic weight. He traced it some 120 meters off to his backward side, without hesitation he spoke another, flew up again to a point over his drowning seedling and cast down his left arm. White-hued arvicity flowed forcefully from his hand and extended onto the lake cutting it into a large open portal of ten meters all around. The left was followed by the right, having already put away the tracking device, and the icy aqua rose in a twisted cylinder drawing all of the liquid out including what one could see as a faint image of Shev'la now disoriented and cold. Another spell held the body up while the aqua crashed down nearly hitting Calil who had almost reached the point. Tulai grabbed his son and carried him over to the lakeshore. Calil came over running but as he ran over the ice it began to shake and he cried out, "Father!"

"Jump, Calil!" his father cried. "Jump!"

Calil leapt high, just enough to reach solid ground but the tremors on the surface increased until finally at the center it shook, split, then exploded in chunks of ice flying everywhere. Tulai drew up an invisible shield, cast a spell to warm Shev'la then readied himself after helping Calil.

"Calil, take your batier," he said while he drew his own long batier. His was black lutium, the hardest of all ceramics, just over a meter in length and rounded like a pole. All entans used batiers in melee but the proficient ones used a handful of moves to win an opponent. As an inventor, Tulai had only mastered the basics of armed combat.

Out from the underneath came a long white beast with gleaming blue scales measuring some twenty meters from head to tail. It leapt out of the cold aqua onto its two oversized front legs and balanced its torso on a flexible fish-like body.

"My lake! My lake!" It roared of definite anger for what was claimed as his and now disturbed. "You puddles of mud. Puddles you are. Puddles you will die!"

Creatures and beings of all shapes and sizes were gifted with the ability to communicate. It was innate in all things living. But those of greater power and ability had higher levels of language. By Tulai's guess, as he was assessing the situation fully realizing that he was not the greatest warrior, this serpentine whale was of greater power than he alone. He and his seeds were in danger.

"Krag—I am Krag! Krag!" he roared once more. "Who are you? Tell me before you die," he demanded in a deafening voice not trained or caring in the level of intonation. Tulai and Calil felt disoriented by the sound. Shev'la started to stir from his cold slumber.

"T-Tulai, Calil, and Shev'la. We did not come to disturb you," Tulai's voice trembled with uncertainty. Creating and warring were diametrically opposed. The inventor's cerbind was weaving a plan. "We will be on our way and leave your place," he said and started to grab his two seedlings ready to exit.

"I am disturbed! You disturbed me—entan! You will feed me now. Feed me your seed, entan. That one over there," he said pointing to Calil with an outstretched clawed hand. "Feed him and I will let you and the other go."

"We have done no wrong here beast. No wrong."

"Feed him or die together!"

Tulai turned his back as if to leave, prepared a spell, turned quickly and cast it out. White sparks flew out from his hand, formed a ball, and graced the air at flamma speed. Krag breathed shards of ice on it which caused it to explode in a noxy ball of fire searing his torso on the left side. He howled and jumped directly in front of the three who now were on the lake shore. Shev'la was still on the ground recuperating. Tulai held both arms out to guard his family. Krag stood seven meters high and as wide as half that. His arms were small hills of hardened flesh. The left hill-sized arm moved quicker than anticipated and grabbed Tulai by both legs. He held him to his face. Calil struck the creature's body with his batier with little effect on the thick scales until after the fifth strike his batier snapped in three. A strange carbonic-yellow liquid oozed out.

"Spell user!" he roared and whose sound deafened Tulai.

Tulai quickly searched for an item from his pocket, got a hold of it tight just as Krag spoke again. Tulai knew that his own arvic lists would not be able to hurt the creature without also hurting him and only wounding it would claim all of their lives.

"Why are you here? Why?!" Krag demanded as if trying to ask a reasonable question.

Tulai, hunched over and seemingly debilitated, pulled out the item muttering a word to command it. The beast heard the sound.

"What did you say?"

"I have a gift for you. Take it!" as he spoke he thrust out a small black spherical device that upon touching his glistening blue scales attached itself and began spinning inward into its flesh. Krag cried in pain and dropped Tulai. The black device bore a hole straight through the creature who was too angered to notice it any longer. Instead, it turned to Tulai again and breathed out a multitude of sharp shards. An arvic shield, encompassing Calil and he, deflected all of the shards, since Shev'la had stealthily maneuvered himself behind the beast onto what was a block of thick translucent blue ice.

The block gave Shev'la strength and fed his arvic talents, taught to him by his father. He called the arvic waves and swirled his imagination and together cast out a blue-hued spell that struck at Krag's back of the head. Krag stopped, groaned, closed his mouth tightly along with his eyes as if his cerbus had been squeezed hard by an invisible palm. Then his head was pulled back into the aqua and his body followed involuntarily. Shev'la dropped for the second time. Tulai and Calil ran over to help him. He had fallen unconscious on a large block, more than three meters in length and two in width. There was a fuzzy bluish shape inside, something modeled after an entan's shape for sure. Tulai felt the presence of ora strong here and the arvic fields around the object were enveloped within themselves suggesting that the arvic power of what was contained in the ice did not belong here or was too powerful for the area to absorb. In any case, his curiosity convinced him to bring it back after helping Shev'la back to consciousness. The rectangular block was moderately heavy but inventors had their ways of moving things about with arvicity and technology combined. Tulai was one such entan and his handy transport stick proved most useful with this unwieldy thing.

No one knew that Shev'la could no longer manipulate arvicity in addition to being afraid of jumping off of heights after that day. When all things were considered and tabulated these minor points would eventually be completely irrelevant.

Nothing was found so easily, Tulai reviewed in his cerbind, that is not meant to be found. Reasons are made for all that is known. Not even Tulai could have guessed the result of his discovery that day on Nivata Lake.

Chapter 6

POOLS OF arvicity swirled this way and that around the diminishing rectangular block of ice as Tulai, focused and intense, rotated his arms as he shaped the cosmic energies. Calil and Shev'la stood at either side though Shev'la had taken several steps closer to the blue being protected from the outside. Or was it the other way around? Young Shev saw the bluish blur inside though could not discern nor judge it.

Command verse came frequently and Shev'la knew their meanings and what was to come but he could no longer manipulate arvicity since the episode at Nivata Lake. Drawing on such great oratic energy at his tender age scarred permanently and forever destabilized his arvic talents removing all chance of arvic casting now and in the future. He had not thought of it much until now as his illness took precedence and occupied all his thoughts. Then when he began to be transfused with Anativo's naqui he became obsessed with it, the feeling of clarity and strength and all things possible, and naqui essence consumed his cerbind. Consumed it deep and he began to dream a new dream full of new possibilities. He began to feel as though he had the capability to control this planet of Seronians, to subdue them, and to take revenge for what they had done to him. Dreams filled with blue skinned beings, Nivians he knew though not completely certain, and betrayal filled his sleep and he would find himself waking bent of destroying those that had hurt him. That had caused him fragrant pain. Sometimes flashes of battles and beauty came to him making no sense as he saw it. The dishonest face of a Nivian female haunted him. But he knew, he had said to himself, that he had accepted much more than just the Nivian's milk, what was inside each of our cerbinds flowed in through our bodies so that all molecular parts felt the truest desires. Molecules interacting with one another. Dancing atoms.

Shev'la felt comfortable and happy this day, not for his father's work, but for the resurrection of the one who gave him life. He had become sicker shortly after the battle with Krag. None of his family had made any connection to the experience with the arvic spell he had cast using the energy of Anativo who lay locked inside. Instead they blamed it on a weak corius from birth and were satisfied or lacked interest for further speculation. But something did happen.

ANATIVO FELT as if a cold veil had been quickly removed from his body and once again he could feel the sting of life's energy and conviction, and how marvelous it felt yet there was something terribly wrong. He couldn't move, locked still by some unknown cosmic force. Flamma be frozen, he thought to himself, and shield me with ice, mother, shield me with ice. Still nothing happened. Mother, where am I? Where have you put me? He wanted to desperately shed blue tears until he realized that he had no eyes with which to reveal such uncommon tenderness. A sharp pain was felt in his formless body and he had no way to soften it's effects. Mother, please find me and shelter me. I am hidden and afraid. Mother! Mother! he cried without a sound coming out and without another to hear him. Mother! he yelled one last time after realizing that still no sound was heard nor had anyone discovered him and finally, without knowing how much time had passed for all was blank and he was unseen, he reached a state of calmness. Of acceptance. Have I become nothing? If it is so then what has been the purpose of finding it? And no answer came; instead, a question arose in him.

"Purpose...your...is...what?" a drum-filled voice asked.

Anativo did not have an answer and became fearful of not having one. He tried desperately to move away from its source but he was dragged closer.

"Purpose...your...is...what?" a drum-filled voice repeated.

"I am my own purpose," he said trying to move away.

"Purpose...is...what?" a drum-filled voice repeated a third time and its drum grew deeper and slower, and Anativo felt what remaining life he had being sucked out from him.

"I am...I am—" he thought as his own thoughts faded to a question he could not answer when suddenly a warm light grew larger behind him and though he could not see, he indeed felt its love and reached out for it. It caught him and pulled, but the drum's rhythm became slower and more powerful.

THE ICE had evaporated now and left behind the remnants of a once great Nivian wounded from battle that had slowly claimed the remainder of his life. Suddenly, Tulai heard a loud clang on the table as if something of dense ceramic had crashed down upon it but nothing was there. Shev'la looked again but still found nothing. His father finally sent out a wave of a white mist designed to stick to all things invisible. On the edge of the table, the mist stuck only for an instant on a long object before disappearing in a vapor. Tulai cast another wave denser than the first and this time when the mist stuck it took shape long enough for all to see what was there.

The mist grabbed the mysterious object trying to prevent its escape once again. Round smooth corners it turned around one end then traced a long shaft nearly a meter and a half in length and as thick as an entan's arm, until it finally reached the other end upon which was fixed a round white ball, no thicker than the rod itself. Before it turned invisible again, Tulai wrapped it in cora silk and locked it away in his hidden safe. As he wrapped it and carried it over he couldn't help to stop the dozens of questions that flooded his cerbind. What was it? Why was it found with the blue being? What was its purpose? Why does it stay hidden? He felt that it had no presence even in his hand as if it was non-existent. As if it existed somewhere else. He would have to study it but should keep it secret for now between him, Calil, and Shev'la.

The body had beautiful blue skin and long white hair now soaked and made dirty with old aqua from the lake. Charismatic squarish-eyes of a piercing orange, just below the hairline and much larger than an entan's roundish eyes, closed and still as if waiting for the dream to end. Sharp facial features ended in a sensual chin, elongated and smoothly shaped as would polished snow. His stylish clothes were not of cora but of ice, yet were soft and firm to the touch and a little chilled. The colors on his suit were mainly white highlighted with blacks and magnetic blues. He had two rings, one on each long-

fingered hand, that bore the symbol of a black spike
pointed skyward. On his right, firmly grasping
something underneath his shirt, was found a white-
lined square on a deep black ring of simple design.
After releasing his right hand, Tulai noticed a shiny
object around his neck and after removing his shirt
he found a black chain ending in a black square
similar in design to the ring and also marked with
an upright spike in blue and white. Upon closer
inspection it was seen that it was indeed to be made
of a form of kium, the densest and rarest of all the
ice. The left ring was blue in color with a short
string of ten small crystals across the top. Tulai
began removing all three items.

Anativo had no weapon of any kind and even
Tulai began to question himself as to what role this
Nivian really played on Nivata. Only some do not
carry weapons on Seranor, he thought to himself,
only some and it is for reasons of ability and nobility.
This Nivian must have reason to escape such a place
given his own power of command over others but his
eyes are not white as are the higher nobles in their
realm; instead, they are orange.

"Is it safe, father?" Calil asked.

"Safe, he is not awake yet," Tulai replied, as he
pulled off the first two rings.

"Maybe he wants to keep them," said Shev'la as if
speaking in defense to the unconscious body.

"Maybe Shev'la, but we have yet to know all of
what he is and why he has come and until that is
made more clear we must have some caution
between us and him," he said while lifting the

Nivian's head and removing the black chain.
"There—finished with that. Now to the other
things...Shev'la, help me to remove his clothes. Calil
get that fresh set of cora silks over there," he said
turning his head from side to side so that both may
hear him clearly. They washed him and then fitted
him with dry cora silks. Tulai had further removed
several vials of naqui and had stored them safely
hoping to use them in his research later on. Shev'la
had become strong and healthy from drinking a
modified and heavily filtered extract of naqui, this
showed promise as a potential source of energy later
on. Now was the time to cast the final set of spells
and to test his ability in Nexitix.

Feeling hot, Tulai removed his outer robe then
walked over to the center ring. He commanded
several verse and a flat bed, the result of combined
rays of white radiation emanated from the air. Then
upon walking back the radiation bed followed and he
directed it, with a fluidic motion of his left palm, to
the unconscious Anativo. The white platform
touched the Nivian's body, went black momentarily,
then disappeared. Tulai called three verses in
succession, the white rays came again surrounding
all parts of the Nivian's body and then slowly
entered his icy skin.

Tulai maneuvered himself around the top of his
motionless head, reached out both hands with the
call of one word, arvicity arched across both hands as
he quickly landed on both sides of his oversized
chest. The body lurched up as did both Calil and
Shev'la.

"He moved!" cried Shev'la.

THE DRUM deconstructed what remained of him, of what he once was, and every beat removed one of the few pieces that still remained. If not for the warmth that had come he would have surely been completely shattered into the emptiness of nothing. The warmth had lurched him abruptly back, sucking him out of the drum's sound, and he slowly began to reform.

Tulai then shifted his right hand to Anativo's head as his body shook violently in arvic waves. He called another verb, different from the rest, and a translucent twisted cord appeared from Anativo's belly that went up into the ceiling.

An invisible cord floated up and poked at Anativo as if put there on purpose and he held on tightly for what it had to offer. The ride had begun.

Tulai was dead focused on his spell and knew that the time now was for the kol, which all beings had, to return. Anativo's kol had left him only partially, making him feel that he had died but uncertain if that was so. The kol hid and Tulai had found it between planums yet named. He called it back and had prepared the body to accept it once more. It made its way quickly through invisible space and Tulai could feel the determination set inside it as if driven by some powerful verdict. Return it did. By the time the ride had ended, Anativo had gone deaf and unconscious to the drum's beat. One hour and forty minutes had passed, about one hour more than expected but given the complexity and the strangeness of the being underneath his hands now, the time was in fact quite short. He stopped, removing his hands quickly from both chest and head, then calling out another word to stop the process which he had started. Calil and Shev'la stood mouth open and wide-eyed the whole time. Shev'la, strange as it seemed, held a tiny smile in the corner of his mouth.

"It is done. It has returned," Tulai said, exhausted from the reanimation process.

"What has returned, father?" asked Calil in a way that sounded apprehensive of what had actually returned.

"His kol. It has returned," Tulai said plainly. Shev'la did not need to ask but felt it. He felt that Anativo had come back to life and he also knew, without a real answer as to what or when, but he knew that Anativo would not keep his name for long. "But this strange invisible device causes my concern."

Tulai looked worn as if by working several days without sleep and minimal food. He had used his theory of reanimation to bring Anativo's kol back thinking that it was what he was obligated to do since if not for Anativo his seed would be dead and his theories unfinished. And yet, in all this contemplation and arvic extraction he thought to himself, why did I have to do it and what have I really done? It was not by accident that Anativo was put here but my family's role was not over just yet

and I now fear that this was only the beginning of
something none of us could control. It—it was done
now. And that could not be changed. The first step
– precursor to all destinations – was done.

Chapter 7

HOURS TURNED to days and days to weeks and still
nothing came of Anativo's reanimation. Polinatum
often came by the unamid to see what had happened
and left disappointed to hear of no news. He had
communicated with the elements; after all he was a
true Sagmal and given the responsibility to carry the
burden of those before him who betrayed Seranor
and caused her enslavement. The elements had
confirmed his suspicions that Anativo was indeed no
accident and had been sent here but they could not
trace nor identify what had created such a window
in history. Perhaps there was none in the design,
only in action.

Tulai, too, began to talk with the elements and began to heavily drink *anaprimo*, the potion of elemental communication, temporarily forgetting his own works in arvicity ever since the day he finalized the resurrection of the blue Nivian. Sometimes he spent days in contemplation and meditation with the elemental forces who told him many things he did not want to hear. They told that he had had no choice in finding or in reanimating Anativo who would soon enough reveal his real name and purpose on Seranor. They told him that energy could only continue and that sometimes it required motivation in the form of desperation to realize what was true for them.

The elements soon came in his dreams and in his waking moments; they came to remind him that he had no choice except to be chosen as the one capable of such possibilities. It was no accident that he had become a Nexitist just as it was no accident that Shev'la had grown sicker. All things were tied to what was yet to come. All things were prepared for what not all could see. And it was their certainty of the matter that scared him the most for it made him realize the ineffectuality of his potential as an entan trying to become more but destined to always remain an entan, a pawn in the scheme of all things in the cosmos. This they did well to remind him that he was just an entan that had given new birth to a king.

Tulai thought, there was no need to concern myself with what I have done. I should consider what else I can do. It was in his nature, a deep-rooted innate ability, to always return to the brightness of subjects and solutions rather than to fall deeper, as many did, into the void of despair, dissolution and discrimination. An entan he was, and not without the truest of gifts. Arvic power, reanimation, fighting and killing, control were all wanted things by many and highly valued by most but he had been given a true gift, next to creation, of seeing the hope in the hopeless.

It was really a matter of perception as he had always seen it. Misperception was the real doom of entans and of Aquanomicus. Inside each of us, he said while thinking to himself, inside each of us is the switch that can see and not see; feel and not feel; react and not react. It is the switch of perception for all entans are already dead unless they can realize that life is unlimited according to the kol inside each and every living being. Life is eternal in the cosmos; and the cosmos is eternal life. Perception he called it. Perception.

Polinatum came by one early morning moving more erratic than normal and speaking in quick tongues and sounding slightly desperate, probably worried about some information he had learned from his commune with the elements. His whitish robes had been messily put on, his hair was much more ragged than normal, and he hadn't bathed this morning surely all signs that something important had been occupying his thoughts. He found Tulai at the front of his residence tilling his garden while whistling a happy tune.

"Tulai!" he said louder than he really wanted but unable to control his emotion.

"Who's that?" Tulai asked without turning from his concentration on pulling out a weed from the cora garden. He had been digging for three hours but weeds had grown from weeks of neglect. "Is that you, Polinatum?"

"Tulai," he said more calmly though still breathing a little heavier than normal from the long walk.

"It is you," Tulai said turning quickly to confirm his guess. "I missed you yesterday as I went out shopping for some materials. Sorry, I wasn't around. Lez told me that you had come by...I'm just in the middle of removing these old weeds from this garden of mine. It seems that if you don't pay attention then things can grow where you cannot see them. Taking them out can be troublesome."

"I was visited yesterday," said Polinatum.

"By whom?" asked Tulai.

"Amid Levin and his seedling, Ira."

"What brings a Kozoty from the north?"

"Your experiment. He knew about Anativo."

"How could he know?"

"House Levin has been responsible for much of the current technology that we use including weapons and information."

"So what did the royal Amid want from us?" Tulai said, sarcastically.

"He did not say in clear words but if I understood him, he came to warn us about Anativo."

"Anativo is fine. He sleeps still. How can he cause any problems?"

"My concerns have grown also, Tulai. And now with Amid in town, surely there will be more. The Nivian is a sign, a mark of change to the planet. Amid believes that it is a mark of our destruction. A zamma ball waiting to explode with the greatest magnitude."

"The Nivian has been brought to us, yes, I agree, but not for reasons of destruction, for reasons of purification. He can help us, old friend. His ideas, his intellect, his ability far surpasses our greatest cerbinds. He can teach us what we have been unable to learn. To help us piece together what we need."

"Life has been stable, Tulai Khan. Life has been good."

"Even you have said that change is a part of life. That change is good. Here is a mark of change. A chance to improve," Tulai said.

"A chance to lose," replied Polinatum.

"Of course there is risk."

"Inventors are born not to see risks. Sagmal are born to protect what is there."

"Again, you remind me of our differences. You must talk with the elements and listen to what they say."

"I have been communicating with the spirits lately and they have revealed something to me that you should know," Polinatum spoke quickly as if it had waited in his head a day too long. He went on. "As you are aware, entans have what is known as

the three perfections – cerbind, corius and kol. We
all have them and is what makes us special to
Seranor."

"Yes, I'm aware of that," he said trying to quickly
confirm his own knowledge and sounding a bit
curious as to where Polinatum was heading in this
talk while still trying to dig out the roots. "It—it's
basic knowledge to us all now."

"But something is different now. Something is
very different. Something is terribly different," he
said with each line heightening in excitement.

"What are you reaching for here?" Tulai asked
trying to calm him down.

"Nivians are different," Polinatum took a breath
and slowed down his speech. "Anativo, the Nivian
that is about to wake up any day now has something
we don't have. It's the fourth perfection."

"The fourth?" Tulai inquired.

"He, they have a fourth perfection that totally
separates us from them. The elements called it the
Vicisso, the amplifier of all responses and
assimilation. The vicisso is unique to Nivians in
that it amplifies and tweaks messages as is needed
to achieve its ultimate goal – control. They could
not—would not tell me, how much messages are
amplified nor what effects would be seen. It is as if
they are created with a genetic tool that can
potentially give them unlimited arvic abilities on
planet Aquanomicus," he went on. "Only the Kozotal
can compare but they have long since been gone
from this place. We are alone. Even the greatest
Arvicians will be no match for one whose arvic

manipulation is amplified to levels none of us have ever seen or dreamed of. Should he continue and gain in full what he had before, his innate programming will make him a god and, I fear, will make us his slaves."

Tulai, while intently listening with his face turned to him, pulled out the weed with all it roots and mud, the green mud sprayed both of them and left marks of green on their white skin and light colored clothes.

"I hadn't considered this," said Tulai, looking at the hole in the ground from the ripped out weed. "This changes what we have done and tried to do."

"You have grown attached to this stranger. I can see that, but when he awakes and realizes why he is here then it will be very late to do anything. Very late," his friend said.

Tulai was thinking of a way to consider this situation properly though none was apparent. If not for Anativo he would have much less than he has now. He owed him his life back. He owed and at the same time he was an entan of Seranor and dear friend to Polinatum who had guided his life for many tios, much more than he cared to remember. His friend was soft at times but that was the gift of all Sagmal, soft in the corius and wiser than a hundred of the wisest entans together simply because of his tenderness and understanding that left him open to all possibilities, ideas, and conclusions. So he had to consider that Polinatum was speaking with such concern indicated that the concern was far more serious than appeared on the surface. What could he do?

"I have not grown attached to him—"

"You have. You are so indebted to him that I don't know if you will consider what I will say next but I want you to understand that this does not come easily from me for I have sworn my life against it," Polinatum said in a voice much more serious and colder than before. "Listen to what I have to say. I will say it only once," he said, slowing down his speech turning his head slightly to the left as if trying to hear something even if no apparent sound was there. Polinatum knew that spirits, especially Nata and Niva, could hear things said but they were not so fortunate to hear things thought so he worried that either of them may be listening to him now and he wanted to speak quickly and hoped that Tulai understood but he was scared that if this information was given to another, or to Anativo, his life and the lives around would be in great danger. And if it were told to the elements, whom he swore not to use violence again, they would cast him out and abandon him on the darkest and loneliest road. He had to be subtle and indirect and only hoped that Tulai would take action from his words.

"Yes—"

"What you have found must be lost forever," the Sagmal said, in plain voice staring intently at Tulai.

"Lost forever?" he asked, looking for confirmation but already knowing the answer.

"Forever," Polinatum replied. He reached out his right hand and touched Tulai on his left shoulder as he had done so when he was much younger than he is now. Tulai became silent and calm as if a subtle spell had been cast but so indiscernible that he could not be certain.

"I will consider what you have said my friend. I will consider it. It must be considered. It will be considered," Tulai said, rambling on as if trying to delay the inevitable decision. Trying to fight it. "Thank you for your wisdom. I have always cherished your friendship. I will consider it but we must first see. We should first see the result and try to learn something of the situation. Mustn't we?" he asked hoping for an answer.

"I have spoken," Polinatum said and turned to leave then briefly stopped after the second step. "Do not wait too long." He knew that given the superior arvic abilities of Nivians and their charismatic nature, the sooner this was done the better. Each day that passed would reduce the chances dramatically. He walked slowly home.

Tulai returned to the task of cleaning up the cora garden and left his thoughts to sort out his apparent problem.

AFTER A short but restless nap on the cora grass, Tulai pulled out a small flask, opened it and consumed a portion of the specially mixed anascal that was inside. He laid back down on his back. The effects came as they always did soothing him first then removing the layers of visual lies that he had so

often believed until finally he could see the
Seranivas and could share in their wisdom. They
came as multi-colored fluorescent beings and sang
their songs of twisted verse. Tulai had learned how
to sing with them in limited form and had also
realized when enough was enough. It was well
known among those who practiced arvic
manipulation that if too many verses were heard by
the inexperienced practitioner then their cerbind
would snap and they would become insane forever
damned to know no more than what they had
learned.

Only one Seraniva had visited him this day and
Tulai saw in the background of multi-hued serpent-
like beasts as if the Seragons of old were dancing
once again in the sky.

"You not the one, not one, not one when it is
done," sang the spirit. "Entan you, no more, no more
than what at core, entan you, just plain you'll
insane; entan makes two and reveals what steals to
make planet new...

"Touch that you found it still around, know that
it there lest it made bare; entan you purpose new,
see ball, twist gate and lock members others take...

"One born, death life, talk birth like knife, feed
fire, stoke flame, just before insane..."

He did not know clearly what they spoke of this
day but he could not forget a recurring pattern in the
sky. A Seragon, long and straight, flew through the
sky until its head grew white and bright forming a
round ball. The rod, thought Tulai. It had become a
rod in the sky. Then a bright flamma ray burst out

from the white ball towards every direction until it finally struck him and blinded him. He reeled back, hands over his eyes, rolling away through the grass until after several rolls he stopped and realized that his eyes were fine and it was the illusion of the Seranivas. The ache in his head was more than usual and he agreed not to take so much anascal next time unless absolutely necessary.

The image of the seragon passed through his cerbind again reminding him of what he had seen to be real. A seragon like a rod bursting flamma in all directions, he thought, could only mean one thing – the invisible rod. Jumping up and brushing his clothes of debris he quickly collected himself and ran towards the chamber. Once there, he rushed over to the safe, opened and pulled out the cora silk-covered object.

"Now we will see what story you have to tell," he said, talking to the object. After placing the invisible rod on the table he cast several spells and images of the rod's past were revealed to him.

The first images showed a realm of bright flamma with flamma beings walking about then the object was taken in flight, stolen by a stranger. All went dark for some time. When the images came back, the object was on a lush blue planet filled with seragons and Nivators who fought a great war in aqua, land and sky. The planet shook again. The image went black. The third time that the images returned, the object was flying through the sky held tight by a winged monster baring triangular fangs from its huge jaw. It flew across many great distances until something was found and the object was used to cut open the planet's surface to expose the head of a great seragon. Once done other objects of various sizes, he counted six or seven in total, cast out their arvic energies upon the serpentine-beast. The humongous beast roared in futile resistance.

When the image returned for the fourth time, Tulai could see a Nivian arvicerer, similar to the one he had found, majestic in stature with arcs of blue arvicity flowing easily from his hands, while holding the rod, and striking those upon the land wiping them clean from the surface all the while laughing at his immortality and as the image went black for the last time he could hear the scream of a once great serpent-being as it became enslaved to form the essence of a planet. He did not realize it but he was crying as if the images had really taken him to those places. "Seven items not six," he said to himself gasping for breath. "Not just one. There is only one ancient set that this can be – the lost Arvinstrum. It is the Arvinstrum. Destiny thickens."

As he examined the rod closely he found seven arvic glyphs permanently embedded into the alien material. Hours had passed before he finally found the spell to make the rod revealed. It grew visible slowly. The rod was a masterpiece in simplicity but designed like no other device he had ever seen. It was the creation of an ancient genius that if the stories were true as he remembered them then it was a Kozotal who indeed was responsible for such an item of creation. Translucent metallic ceramic made up its main piece, smooth and warm to the touch, leaving no mark or stain as if nothing had ever touched it. As if it recreated itself simultaneously and continuously. The Kozotal were the beings of creation from the planet of Flamma and this was one of their finest examples of work. At the end of the silver rod was fitted a ball, white in color but lacking in substance when touched.

There was no other way to know its true power unless tested for the Kozotal had hidden its abilities deep in a place he could not find. Normal arvic devices could be identified in all their abilities with spells to do so. But this rod would not so easily divulge such information, so the other way to know it would be to test its power. Tulai went out across several kilometers, while Lez·win and his two seedlings were gone, to a place barren except for a couple of small hills and some patches of young cora trees. He removed the rod from his pack, prepared some spells so that he may identify its full power, then held it fast in both hands. "All shall be revealed," he said with no one there to hear him.

A short command was heard before the white ball at the end of the rod increased in brightness and then from its face burst force a brilliant flamma ray curved and sharp as it pierced the land. Bright flamma spewed everywhere and Tulai was blinded temporarily; he only could hear the sounds of sharp tears through rock and clay as the ground beneath him shook lightly. By the time he opened his eyes, he could not believe what had been done. The ground in front of him spanning several hundred meters in both directions to his left and right had been cut into a chasm about ten meters wide and, to his best estimate, half a kilometer long. The Rod of Carving, now he knew, was that what he had found from the frozen Nivian. It was called Seca and was possessed at the time of Seragorn's enslavement when Nivians and Karul caught Seragorn, trapped her and forever locked her.

The chasm ran deeper than fifty meters and a cool breeze arose from it. Tulai sat near the edge contemplating what his next move should be and how he was going to hide this from the unconscious Nivian in his chamber. In his distractions, he did not see that the release of such tremendous amounts of arvicity sent an arvic pulse towards the town that ran through the chamber and resonated through the blue being on the table.

Chapter 8

MAREENTH LAZPUL held innocent beauty in her bosom like a flower in the cora fields on a warm afternoon under the blue skies caressing you with kindness as wind breezed softly on the tender cora flesh. She had come from Casus, the wellspring of all that was considered to be the place of total adventure, real and unreal. It was the greatest urba, at least most famous if not most perplexing, that many a young luto often ventured to in search of making their wills sincere, and in the end adding their name to the lost generation of statistical quotients, Generation Q, namely lutos and lutas who had deemed themselves worthy of greatness and

ending into a range of entan statistics from the
materially wealthy to the irrevocably dead.
Mareenth herself was part of Ques Generation,
though she had tried to make her mark she soon
discovered herself and removed her life from that of
Casus whose inhabitants had become somewhat
more vulgar, more possessed and more productized
than the rest of a peaceful planet. Casus became the
place where all things were possible and impossible.
It was an urba of trichotomy.

Mareenth, at a young age, became involved with
the Karul traders who sold karuli as sex slaves to
the growing luto of wealth in the urba. Although she
was not a karuli herself, she had been enticed at a
young sexual age and grew to like having mysterious
sex on a weekly and daily basis. Her trader, Cosm,
treated her well by providing the right food and
clean living conditions. All of them lived in a
trilamid which housed a hundred or so sex slaves in
their own cells. Cosm lived outside in his own
residence. He wore short blue hair and was
extremely fat, made of what seemed like reams of
soft blue mud though smooth to the touch. Sensual
to some. His enormous size, almost twice that of any
luto in three directions, made it a challenge for he
himself to engage in sexual activity but karuli were
not ones to discriminate. They were highly sexual in
nature and simply enjoyed the activity sharing little
emotion in the process. Cosm was an interesting
partner to have. Karul were generational
descendants of Nivians who once lived on Seranor

and still had some of their gifts though none could compare to true Nivians.

Leaving Casus was difficult for Mareenth. She had made many friends, among them those that were her sexual partners, and enjoyed the extremes that could be found in the urba. Things started to change, or at least she saw things differently, after her karuli friend Bia was killed by a Malkar. It had called itself Jod and been disguised as a plain a luto as any. Bia was sweet and had become inattentive over the tios thinking that nothing would happen since nothing had ever happened. She had had some strange partners but nothing to threaten her life with. Jod was entirely different. He came in crying that he had lost something important to him as if the whole planet had stolen from him and wanted to be with Bia. Soft and tender he was for a couple of hours until Seranor awoke early in the morning, without wrong or reason he turned cold on Bia breaking her arm with one fell swoop from a fist. She had run out of her cell screaming in fear and Mareenth had run to meet her seeing her milk running out profusely from her cracked skin.

"What happened?! What happened?!" she remembered yelling until the answer came down the hallway and as Jod came walking he turned into brown mud thick in all directions. His true face was revealed – a Malkar pure as pure it can be. Jod went on a rampage and killed a handful of karuli simply for pleasure, or sport as evidenced from his laughter. Cosm wasn't able to kill Jod but used his arvic abilities to sting him enough so that he left. In reality, Jod wasn't so much hurt as he was bored of killing the helpless.

Mareenth left Casus the next day. She wandered for several weeks until she found the garden of all gardens in the town of Ulaq, not more than ten kilometers from Nivata Lake. She fell in love with the calmness and inner beauty of the city longing more for peace and quiet from the life she had led previously. It was on her first day in the town that she had met Shev'la. He was on his way to the center to order some washing soap for the household as it had run dry. Shev'la was weak that day, probably from the effects of his chronic illness, and felt unmotivated to do things. He had left the house unwillingly and angrily because his mother ordered him to go. She didn't like to do that but he had been in the house for a week feeling more and more depressed as each day passed. Shev'la's moods shifted up and down at unpredictable times. It was a combination of both not wanting to see him like that and hoping for better things outside that she forced him to go out for the most frivolous of items. A change of scenery couldn't hurt. They didn't really need soap, his mother always kept extra packages hidden around the house, even Shev'la knew that. He understood that he had to get out too so he agreed.

Mareenth had first approached Shev'la in the street looking like the lost stranger she was at the time.

"Excuse me, can you show me how to go to the town center?" she asked politely with an exaggerated smile on her face.

Shev'la didn't speak rather he pointed his hand in the general direction.

"That way?" she asked trying to confirm.

"Well, look at my hand!" he blurted out. "Where else is it pointing?" He kept walking until he was past her. She stood briefly, confused at his impoliteness then pressed her mouth together mumbling the line Shev'la had just blurted. He stopped dead in his tracks and turned around after hearing it with his superb hearing.

"What did you say? Are you looking for trouble luta because I can show you trouble."

"What way is that to treat a luta?"

"My way. Okay?"

"No, NOT okay. Okay?"

"What is your problem today? Are you lost?"

"My problem is you. And yes, I am lost, thank you."

"Well, why are you lost?"

"Because I have never been here and the luto here are not at all friendly."

"Really, not friendly. How can that be? Maybe we should open up a bureau for all the strangers that come here."

"Maybe, you should just be more polite to ceramin."

"I am polite."

"You are an impolite Malkar!" she said, loudly and turned to walk away.

Shev'la was stumped for she was right. His poor health had infected his cerbind and his manners more deeply than he realized. He could only imagine the strain on his mother recently. This luta was right, he thought. I am a Malkar. What is a Malkar? But I shouldn't have treated her like that. Stupid me. I hate this illness. I wish it would kill me sooner rather than later. Damn! He noticed that she was headed in the wrong direction.

"You're going the wrong way!" he yelled, no response was seen so he ran up to her. "Stop! Please, I'm sorry…the town center is over there," he said pointing again in the general direction. The run, along with the talking, drained him of energy and he felt the numbness coming. He tried to delay it. "It's that way."

"Now you want to help me. Now you want to help," she said sounding belittling.

"Anyway, it's over there," he said, gasping for a breath and seeing his vision blurring until all became dark like several times before.

"Where did you go? Hello? Wake up? Somebody help!" she cried, then ran to get help from a nearby luto who knew of Shev'la and his crazy father. They took him to his residence. An hour later Shev'la had regained consciousness. He awoke to again see the beautiful luta in his sight, and in his dream she was there to stop his fall into a place where everything was still and nothing existed. She was his savior.

"Did you find the center?" he asked.

"No. Not yet," she said, smiling that he hadn't died.

"I'm sick, you see," he said.

"I know," your mother told me about it. "Are you feeling strong now?"

"I never feel strong but I will be all right for now," he said slowly and without energy.

"Shev, you have to be more careful when you go out. You can't treat your mother like this. This is awful for me," Lez-win said, holding back red tears until her eyes glistened. She brushed his hair. "This nice luta found you." Well, actually he thought, it was because of this luta that I am like this but let's not get into that.

"Yes, she did find me," he said, smiling a faint smile with a look of a deeper meaning in what they had truly found.

"I have to go now," Mareenth said feeling a little uneasy with Shev'la's smile, not ready to start any kind of relationship, not even knowing what she would do in this little town.

"See you again luta," he said then realized that he did not know her name. "What is your name?"

"It's Mareenth...Mareenth Lazpul," she said while briefly stopping, placing her left hand on her left hip and leaning beautifully to one side, and keeping only enough time to speak her words and then exiting the front portal with quick steps and graceful body movements.

It was the first time they met and the beginning of a close friendship. Mareenth was never willing to go beyond this friendship barrier for she feared of losing Shev'la to his debilitation which she had, at times, difficulty making up her mind about since she began to care for him so. When he was feeling strong she moved herself closer to his life and when he weakened she cast herself away and each time she pushed away it became increasingly difficult to return to the same closeness. He was dying and made it clear to her as he did his love for her and his hope that all would work out. But as time passed, Shev'la became weaker and closer to death. And their friendship became further and further apart. It was the best position in absolutely the worst situation and neither of them grew to like it; instead, they grew disdain for it and all the horrible memories it brought along with it.

LUNCH WITH Mareenth and her flowing black hair and sparkling black eyes was a delight that Shev'la took great pleasure in. No matter which eating den they entered Mareenth was the firelight that burned a memory space in those she passed as she walked by their tables. She always wore tight fitting cora silks of the snazziest colors and spoke with a confident but semi-sensual allure that most luto were sure to be charmed by.

"Two will be eating and not more than two," she said to the short-haired and young host at the entrance. A momentary blank expression fell upon his face. "Two for eating, remember?" she said, trying to get his attention.

"Oh yes—uh...yes, two right – right over there. Here is your disk and happy eating," he said and handed a round but flat ceramic disk to Mareenth. This was the standard *esaka*, known as the eater's card, and used internally for all eating dens, *eadens*, so that all patrons could comfortably and quietly order what they wanted. The clay food was cooked in or on flammic ovens designed to cook with the exact amount of heat necessary to render the clay edible while still preserving all of the original nutrients and even enhancing some of the nutritive functions within the food. Orders were given into the esaka and this was placed into the table's side and fitted into a special slot to accept it. This information was then transferred by photon rays to the central kitchen information receiving area and relayed to a particular chef who would oversee the cooking process. Flammic ovens were encoded with arvic glyphs to respond exactly to orders received and patrons had all learnt the most basic cooking commands and procedures. Those of a higher society grew very particular tastes for particular foods and how they were prepared and so used special commands suited to their diets. It was an efficient and cleanly basic system that all Seronians followed.

After placing their orders and inserting the esaka into the slot, Shev'la looked around the cell, not wanting to look Mareenth in the eyes.

"Shev'la? You are thinking of something, I can tell," she said casually. He raised his eyebrows.

"I am? I was just going to say that you and I have been together for 20 tios now and many things have happened," he said while still looking down at the table and thinking of how he was going to get to the topic of marriage this afternoon. "Together, I mean, that we have been close, sometimes very close."

"Sometimes not so close," she reminded him with innocent eyes hoping that he wouldn't be thrown off by her shallow remark.

"True, but—but there is something special between us," he said, stressing the word "is". He thought quickly to himself, now is the time to say it Shev'la. Don't think about it. You know that it's right. She's the one.

The last time he wanted to marry her he was too sick and too afraid to ask knowing full well even then that she would refuse him. Then he started drinking the milk potions and grew stronger only to see Mareenth caught up with interest over Romal, a two meter tall luto with cropped hair at the ear level and white skin without a blemish to be seen. He was a pure one it seemed, perfect to every detail, healthy, smart, and with a vision of his future. At the time, Shev'la was sickly and dying so the choice was very clear. Romal loved Mareenth much more than she ever realized and she grew torn between the two lutos.

It was on the week that Romal asked her to marry him that Shev'la came to find her. His health had improved after taking his father's potion along with his mood which had sunk to its lowest point prior to that time. She became hopeful again and not wanting to make a wrong decision she decided to be with Romal without marriage for a while and then decide later. Meanwhile, Shev'la recuperated, drew up all his strength and eventually returned to

greater than full. His skin's color changed to a
slightly blue-hued white along with streaks of blue
in his hair. He couldn't ask her to marry him while
she stood with Romal as that was against the
Seronian love habits though some chose to ignore it.
And then seven and a half weeks ago, just about the
time that Anativo was reanimated, she left Romal
but he was too preoccupied with the Nivian to even
think about Mareenth. Still anxiously waiting for
Anativo to awake he found the courage and the
moment to return to this topic.

"Of course, you're special to me," she reiterated.

"I feel that you and I should be more. I want to be
more. I have dreams Ree. Dreams to be more than
what I am. It has been many tios since I've had
these dreams and since I've been sick I never
thought that they could be realized," he said, looking
at his hands playing with the table. "It's just that—"

The dishes came and were placed neatly on the
table along with the utensils to eat them with. Two
transparent and finely-made porcelan goblets filled
with aqua-based anascal arrived at the table. They
each grabbed a goblet and toasted to their
friendship.

"As I was saying Ree, it's just that now I can see
my dreams more clearly, much more clearly now
and—"

"Shev! Shev! Shev, where are you?!" a voice cried
out from the front of the eaden. He looked over,
slightly frustrated at being interrupted twice during
his private talk with the luta he loved. "Shev!
You've got to come," said Calil as he approached the

table breathing heavily as he had run straight from
their residence.

"What is it? What? I'm in the middle of
something important," he said squeezing his mouth
together to prevent himself from shouting.

"He's awake," Calil said. "He's awake now.
You've got to come."

"Yes," Shev'la stood up immediately. "Sorry Ree,
I have to go," he said looking at her. "I—we—"

Off the two went running back to the unamid.
When they arrived at the back where the chamber
was, Anativo was already up and walking outside.
He was magnificent. Calil and Shev'la had never
seen anything like that before. His magnetic blue
hair shown like a mirrored curtain and had grown
long to the middle of his back, his skin radiated
charm and demanded sincerity, and his eyes, oh his
eyes, had become transparent as if looking in them
would swallow your kol. The cora silk fitted him
well but were far beneath the quality that he had
grown accustomed to on his planet. He seemed
rather quiet, probably from the disorientation
associated with what he had gone through, felt
somewhat calmer than expected. Polinatum and
Tulai were there as was Lez-win along with two
strangers and a seedling that the brothers hadn't
seen before.

"Does he speak gutra, father?" Calil asked.

"Yes, and more," he replied. "Anativo, these are
my two seedlings, Calil and Shev'la." Tulai pointed
at the two of them. "It was Shev'la who found you in

Nivata Lake. Without him we wouldn't have survived."

"Shev'la, ruler of serpents, I am indebted to your fate," Anativo spoke slowly and manipulated the pronunciation with such precision that simple words sounded majestic. "It is odd it seems that I am here because of you and equally odd that you are here because of me." His words left Shev'la speechless and no answer seemed relevant enough to match what he had just shared with him.

Nivians were superior to entans, it was certainty. Their cerbinds were not grown but were crafted with divine hands. He held natural charisma and more importantly moved with such fluidity that it commanded respect and attention. Anativo kept his given name for he had forgotten his past; he did not know who he was but only had vague memories of his previous self.

"You saved my Shev'la," repeated Tulai. "And now we are all together again."

"Tell me Anativo, what do you remember of your past? Do you know who you are?" asked Polinatum. He wanted to know, to see if there was chance that his theory was right. Tulai was too happy or more probably proud of his accomplishments to even think about this. Sometimes he was blinded by what he believed to what was in the real. Polinatum was not so single-minded and was open to possibilities as all things were in the elements. The elements were used to create life, to sustain its creation.

"I remember pain and suffocation but it was an internal pain sharp as the sharpest rader that bore into the deepest part of me that I could not defend. I remember this…and I see a grand castle fixed in position and the face of a female I do not remember and if I think of them I do not understand and it perplexes my intellect to be challenged for such small things…my past whatever may be is in my past and now I have been given a new life and a chance to build a story to what I am…" He went on. "What you have done will always be remembered, what I am will be reconstructed and I seek your assistance in this respect once again knowing that I can play my role, a significant role, on your planet. I am dedicated to what I will be."

Anativo was truthful to what he had said and indeed had forgotten what was done to him. In fact, he chose not to think about it any longer. He wanted to retrieve himself and reach his new purpose in his new life. While the others continued to talk, Anativo didn't care to listen and; instead, only sat and watched at the wonder of Seranor. The air was warm to his skin. Still it was comfortable. He waited until some of the others had left.

"It will require him some time to readjust and to redefine himself in the new environment," said Tulai.

"What can we do?" asked Ossas, the third member and another clean white-skinned, well-dressed luto.

"It has been done," said Amid, the quiet stranger. "Soon there will be much to do."

"We must first wait." said Tulai. "Redefinition will take time as he adjusts to the planet surroundings, our culture, and our way of doing things."

"You are an optimistic fool, Tulai. It is in a fool's folly to do such things without regard for the greater consequences," said Amid, annoyed at Tulai's persistence. "You push and push without seeing where you are going."

"Amid, please…" Amid Levin left with his seed.

"He is a kozoty. They are born to hate and mistrust the Nivians and all related to them," said Ossas.

"But they are also gifted my friends and his words may have significance at a later time," added Polinatum.

"Anativo will only need to redefine himself. There will be phases of pleasure and disorientation but given his high intelligence, I think that it won't take him long at all."

"How long?" asked Ossas.

"I estimate about 20 to 30 tios."

Chapter 9

THANKS TO the possibility of directly testing his
theories of reanimation, Tulai was able to
immediately return to the work of finishing his
manuscript, based on his experience on raising
Anativo. When he searched for Anativo's kol, he had
found it immaterially subjected to deafening waves
of sound whose wavelength stretched and grew
stronger as it expanded. It surely was the death
drum to Anativo's final fragments as a stable form of
energy. Every wave of sound that passed knocked
the very cellular binding that contained the material
of the kol. Had he not protected himself with
customized spell lists he too would have been

defragmented. The master of Nexitix hypothesized that sound of an infinite wavelength, not possible from Seranor, stretched the kol as it vibrated through it and pulled at its atomic seams. Despite a Nivian's greatness they were essentially, Tulai guessed, made of the same kol material since the source of all was the same. He had yet to find the true source and still could not understand all the details of the structure of the Versos and its role in relation to planet Aquanomicus. More research would be needed, he smiled a defeated smile.

An uneventful and dreadfully quiet month had passed after Anativo was revived. He remained conserved, probably from still gathering his energy and acclimatizing to a new planet, and fascinated by the ceramin's kindness found in Ulaq. Tulai invited him to a personal tour of his chamber of experiments and introduced him to the variety of inventions and devices he had been forming. The inventor had created the inscriptor to translate spoken verse into elos. And he had found a way to contain elos in a roughly shaped cora ball to make some kind of information dissemination medium. Other parts and pieces for a transmission-reception system based on a crystal inset into a lutium square were strewn about.

Anativo asked, "What is the purpose of this technology to communicate? Can you not communicate without such devices?" Nivians had innate abilities of distant communication.

"No. Not distant communications. Only interpersonal. I see it as a stumbling block for

Seronians. Imagine if everyone carried a small transmitting device then we could all be in contact with one another at anytime," Tulai responded. "Shev'la, in fact, was far more interested in communications. I am only working on standardizing the technology so that it can become widespread.

"My immediate interest, besides Nexitix which I have mentioned to you in brief, is in transport. That is another societal problem. Why do we need to physically walk to buy things or travel long distances? We shouldn't have to. Just like an Arvician who can throw a spell, I am working on a smaller device like this one," he held up a flat disc with glyphs along the bottom, "that can essentially flash inorganic products from one place to another."

"And what about organic things?"

"That is more difficult. There is a crossing of wavelengths and it interrupts the matrix structure causing assimilation then degradation and this...oh, listen, I must apologize because if we start on this technical stuff I can go on endlessly. Why don't I show some other inventions of mine and see what sparks fly inside of your head..."

Anativo took to the tour with great interest and Tulai, for the first time, felt that here was someone who could appreciate his inventions.

CONSIDERING ANATIVO'S higher intellect and greater understanding of the Versos, he would wait for the moment when the Nivian could assist him in grasping the intelligence he lacked and needed to finish his anativical theories. He thought of getting Anativo more involved with his work in the hope that details could then be siphoned out simply from exposure to the material at hand. Tulai was expecting Polinatum to visit this evening to discuss more about their theories and ideas and had invited Anativo to the casual meeting. Anativo was more than interested and said that he would join them though not certain how he would fit in the discussion.

Having already spent the greater part of the day contemplating his life in the cora fields, Anativo headed towards the residence of Polinatum, and after entering through the back gate, went to visit the two of them with the intention of politely declining their offer; but they were so welcoming that he couldn't say no. Polinatum, a Sagmal tested in the ways of the elements, and Tulai, who brought the learning of cosmiscience to the region, were trying to better appreciate the misunderstanding between their differing philosophies on the relationship with the Versos and its birth. The Sagmal was carrying on a lengthy debate against the theory of immortality, which Tulai followed with respect and interest; after listening and learning from the Sagmal for decades he had often challenged him with his objections and alternative theories. Polinatum had insisted to continue the discussion to an important question: Was there such thing as the

Versos and what was the role of planet
Aquanomicus?

Tulai greeted his latest project with the same
enthusiasm that he took to all things he did, pulled
over a chair for his new friend, and continued the
conversation with Polinatum.

The Sagmal broke off the discussion for a moment
to welcome Anativo, then went on speaking without
looking at Anativo who sat down in politeness. As
he heard their discussion his interest grew.

Anativo had recalled some innate knowledge that
he had ever since his existence began some time ago
that even he couldn't, at this point, remember, and
which was becoming more clear as the two of them
so fervently spoke about it. He knew the Versos and
all things related to it since he himself was born
with the purpose of controlling the Versos and all
things contained in it. It was his birthright he
recalled in the shape of a passionate pulse but his
attachment to this feeling remained indifferent and
separated from it.

Listening closely to their conversation, he realized
that they discussed concepts of an elemental nature
and of a science, and though he knew of the
elements, he was of science and mathematics and all
their relatives, so each time they tried to resolve
theories of elements and scientific nature there could
not be a compromise, as the view was made from a
different set of beliefs, and when they reached this
point of no compromise they would retreat into the
finer questions of the specifics of measurement,
historical bases, and hallucinatory phenomenon

which Anativo thought was only prolonging a short discussion.

"It is simply a mistake," said Polinatum, with his gentle approach to disagreement. "It is incorrect to think that the world is unitary in nature. The existence of the elements suggest that not only is the cosmos multidimensional but also whose origins are beyond our current perceptions."

"Yes, but you assume that there in fact is a cosmos that we exist in and that can be perceived, as you would say, and that that perception would be available if we could extend our abilities. My theories suggest that the cosmos is just a perception rather than a measurable reality that we coexist with," said Tulai.

"Science is only concerned with measurement and does not—is not capable of perceiving beyond its level of technology or development, yet elemental knowledge says that seeing is not believing, rather the feeling is the result," said Polinatum, but at that point of having mentioned science something stirred in Anativo and he quickly responded on his own merit.

"I have only known science," started Anativo, "for it was taught to be the structure of all things inside and outside of the Versos, so my view is only that of science and I defend neither at this point in time. Science is like a rader—"

"Sorry, Anativo," Tulai interrupted. "You had mentioned this word before but I am afraid that we are not familiar with it."

"Which word?"

"Rader. What is this, rader?"

"It is a ripping weapon, killing if you will; four blunt blades, wide at the hilt and ending in a sharper point." His hands moved to demonstrate and an image appeared in front for them to examine.

"Seronians use batiers," said Tulai, after understanding the superior killing potential of their warring weapon. "Batiers are best suited against clay and ceramic unless embedded with...ah...but please, go on. War is not our interest here."

"The rader is unlike your batiers," Anativo continued, "which subdue mostly and also can kill when necessary. No, the rader in Nivian hands can barrel through an opponent and, as it does so, it rips into flesh sending them to death. I have seen your weapons here and they strike me as odd until I recognize your limits to the materials upon your ground. You see, raders are only made of kium, a super ice that is abundant on the planet from which I came.

"As I have said," Anativo moved to continue while adjusting his halation to get back to his former topic, "science is like a rader. A kium rader is composed of the basic chemical elements of kium which include – at the atomic level – carbon, protein, and trace elements that I will not get into. If you pull out one of the chemical components, the rader is no longer of kium because it will have been changed into something else. The Versos is like this."

Polinatum was offended at first from what Anativo had said, feeling disappointment at what the Nivian had to offer and trying to understand that it was still early. But Tulai, who spoke of a similar, still underdeveloped scientific basis, and had interest to learn more about the Nivian's thoughts, smiled and said:

"Tell us more about Aquanomicus and the Versos..."

"Aquanomicus, if I am correct, is centered in one of the cosmic Versi," he continued. "There are sixty-four Versi and the Versos that we now exist in is the thirty-ninth. Planet Seranor, as you refer to it, is the balance that holds this Versos together and it is what we Nivians and those called the Kozotal have waged war against, and is also why you are here. Losing the balance, to one side or the other, on Seranor will seal the fate of the Versos that will reverberate across the cosmic pool."

"We don't keep the balance. It is Seranor and Seragorn who maintain all things and give us aid with the help of the elements," said Polinatum, defending what had been taught to him from a young age about the true source of power on the planet.

"Misconceptions can run into danger and from this conception of planet Seranor we can be led to believe that she can be eternal and forever the protector of Seronians and all life contained therein, for all time without measure." Anativo went on. "Yet if Seranor and Seragorn are truly in control, as it may be said, then why is it that the simple concept of arvicity that runs in pools and rivers throughout the planet, why is it that this simple yet advanced energy source is limited and can be used to control

Seranor herself given enough of it." Anativo could
see by the open-eyed expressions that his two
companions had not been aware of this most simple
of facts and decided not to push the envelope too far
on this day.

Silence.

"I saw three statues," Anativo started again, "in
the center of Ulaq this morning. One was colored,
one gray with wild hair, and one was white. Are
these your heroes of Seranor?"

"No, Anativo. They represent the cornerstones of
Seronian thought," answered Tulai. Anativo still did
not understand. "The colored statue is of Art. The
gray one with the uncultured hair is Philosophy, and
the white represents Flamma. Every urba and town
has such markings."

"What was the cornerstone of Nivata, Anativo?"
said Polinatum.

"The four rules if I remember: law, politic, science,
and...military. The rules of control and..." A wave
of images and knowledge flashed through Anativo's
cerbus overwhelming him and his current weak
state. He closed his eyes and calmed his excited
breathing. "I am feeling somewhat dislodged from
my recovery so I will venture back and restore my
energy..."

"Yes, please rest if it makes you feel more
comfortable," said Tulai, concerned about his friend.
"There is plenty chance to talk later."

"Grand evening," said Anativo.

They both had stopped, then stood up to show
Anativo off before considering whether or not to

discuss this new and most important information. After Anativo had gone, Tulai turned to Polinatum.

"It was good that he came. His ideas—I've never heard them before."

"They are not those taught by the elements who rule this planet, Tulai. We shouldn't preclude all of our own observations and perceptions from one short meeting. He is a Nivian after all," said Polinatum. "And we, we are elemental."

Tulai wanted to tell his friend and respected elder about how Anativo had helped piece together some of his own ideas, and had knocked open another closed portal in his cerbind, but after listening to Anativo speak about his understanding related to the Versos, and seeing his Sagmal friend so disinterested in what he had to say he felt that the time would come later when they could speak more clearly about it. That time was not this evening.

ANATIVO AND Tulai began spending more time together during the progression of the Anativical Theorem. Tulai began to test his theories and concepts of reanimation against the secure scientific knowledge contained, often hidden, inside of Anativo's cerbind. Tulai couldn't help to wonder about what Polinatum had told him from a long time before about the possibility of Anativo achieving an extreme level of power unmatched by any other being on Seranor from the unknown function of the vicisso. As of yet, there was no sign or indication that Anativo had this function or whether or not it was in use. He would often ask Anativo about it with no clear conclusion as to what was happening, since Anativo himself did not know.

Late one morning, Anativo decided to join Tulai in the arvic chamber, and to get closer to the current project he was working on, but after not finding Tulai inside he decided to wait which eventually caused him to occupy his time, and he did so by reading the manuscript on the table and studying it intently while sitting in the torq of Seranor.

Anativo thought to himself that if it were possible to reanimate a being to remove mortal limitations then it was possible to reverse the process to uncover who he really was. The question was how to do it efficiently and without danger. Who am I? he thought. This question had been burning in his cerbind since the day of his return. Both Tulai and Lez-win had been kind and generous introducing him to all the intricacies of Seronian life. They taught him to eat the many varieties of clay though Anativo could only eat a modified and frozen form of it, to respect individuals, and to have love for that was what contained all life in ecstasy. Love was a concept that was difficult to measure and; therefore, impossible for him to fully grasp no matter how hard he tried. And Anativo was adept at learning, in fact so fast that he learned everything that was said and shown to him like a windstorm that sucked everything up in its path and consumed it in an instant, soon ready for more. Anativo learned well and the more he learned the more he wanted to learn about himself and who he really was. After several hours, Tulai returned to find him in a calm, meditative state. He purposely banged some equipment to make some noise to which Anativo instantly responded to.

"Ah, you are hiding in the chamber," he said. "It is quite relaxing in here. It is so peaceful sometimes and is where I do most of my creative work," he was putting away some things and placing them on the shelves. "What did you think of the manuscript?" he pointed to his hand. Anativo still retained the manuscript in his hand.

"It is well developed friend Tulai but it is missing something critical along with errors in several places," said Anativo without having had a chance to think of a better route than just the direct one. Tulai's face began to glow red in anger after hearing a poorly executed critique of his most important work and that which saved Anativo was wrong or had errors.

"Tulai, do not misunderstand me. I only wish to be direct with you on this manner and there are some technical errors that should be corrected," he said trying to explain his comment. "The critical element, I must consider, for I have not traced its exact point."

"What errors?"

"To suggest that the kol is from outside the Versos is simply wrong. There is nothing outside the Versos except a cosmic meta-molecular gel within which the pool is contained and kept stable. I do not know how you found my kol, for perhaps you were fortunate to find me not completely dead, and my guess is that you found it still on this planum, but should I have died it would have returned to planet Nivata I assure you for kols return to the birthplace of existence."

"And—"

"Another error is that, as you already know, all kols belong to either opus or ora. Kols of opus will travel back to Ingratuum'inus. Oratic kols will return to Nigratuum'inum. This is the stable quotient that you come close to mentioning but it is guaranteed unless prevented from doing so or if it has not finished its time on its birth planum. This I have yet to estimate myself."

"What more can you know about reanimation, Nivians have only known decimation..." he said then realized that what he said was inappropriate and tried to retract it. "I've said too much."

"No, you have said it right. Nivians are like this...but...I am not and I wish you could see that," he said.

"It was irresponsible of me to say so. Let us start again."

"I also have been irresponsible. You have returned me whole again, taken me into your family, and I should not continue like this—it is not as others have shown me. There is so much love in the Seronians of this place and it is the one thing I cannot grasp as if I am born to bow to it rather than capture it whole and bury it in my breast," he said as crystal blue tears swelled in his clear eyes while thinking about friends who loved, kissed, hugged,

and cried together and calling to cerbind that sharp
pain in his chest, that kium spike still thrust deep
from a time that he could no longer make out in
detail. Why have I been denied life's ecstasy? he
thought. Why me?

"You must give yourself time, Anativo. All things
are revealed in time and it is the one thing that is
most difficult to manipulate. We are only able to
manage it and some even fail at that."

Anativo left the manuscript behind and walked
out into the streets thinking to himself. Lute would
walk by and greet him, some were suspicious, but
most were open and gentle. On his way out among
the inhabitants he decided to walk along the cora
fields to gather his thoughts and to calm himself.
While walking softly in the cool grasses, he noticed a
couple happy together and he wanted to see much
closer to understand what is was like to be so close.
He considered it and then as if by some strange hand
his vision began to shift and move towards the
couple yet his body remained. He took delight in it
and sent this visionary eye out to see what love was
all about. His vision reached a large set of cora
trees, the doubly twisted trunks harmonized
together and in the thick of the small cora forest he
found a couple making love. They were beautiful
naked as soft white porcelan. One of the bodies had
a perfect white texture, smooth and silky to the
touch with cropped black hair. The other, a luta,
had roundly shaped breasts, thick buttocks and
whose skin was slightly paled and marked in several
small spaces. Her long black hair caressed the luto.

Anativo shifted his arvic vision and began to feel
disgust as he realized that the luta was Lez-win with
a luto he did not recognize but suspected, because of
his skin, that he might be connected to Ossas, the
nobler of the town inhabitants. At the moment he
lost concentration, the vision disappeared and he left
the area in fear of being caught.

Lez-win had grown lonely over tens of tios with
Tulai's incessant need to work and the pressure of
her sickened Shev'la, and she sought compassion
elsewhere. It was when Mareenth discarded Romal
that his coriatic pain forced him to search for
another to fill his loneliness and he found comfort
and similarity in Lez-win. Tulai did not know, nor
suspect, especially after Anativo came out from his
deep coma which kept him even more preoccupied
and made it easier for her to find solace in Romal's
arms. It was normal for a luta to feel the pain of
emptiness more so than a luto might for his needs
were more simple and crude but lutas needed depth
of love and the warmth of compassion, and this could
quickly be found in a lover's arms though it was also
quick to dissipate requiring an increase in the
dosage as time passed with greater addictiveness
and separation from what she once was. Lez-win did
not think of such things for she had grown so lonely
that it mattered not what or whom she did it with
but it was most important that she tried to fill that
emptiness inside. Romal only wanted sexual comfort
to hide his truest insecurities – he could not show
compassion nor did he care to show it and it was this
fault that made him lose the luta that he loved most,

and when Mareenth accepted his ineptitude she left him lonely and bare as a broken cora tree whose intertwined trunk had been un-spun in a moment's action.

Lez-win did not think to tell Tulai. It had never occurred to her to do such a thing, probably also because she had never been caught although Romal mentioned at one of their sexual meetings that it would be easy to tell Tulai if she chose not to see him anymore. At the time, she had no intention to stop so didn't consider the result of those actions but had she considered it she would have realized that it would be a most ungrateful day and that Romal had a truly unremarkable side to his character that may be his undoing one day.

She returned to the unamid later that day, freshly washed as the day she was born and greeted Anativo in the kitchen.

"What keeps you in the house?" she asked while putting away her things.

"Requirement," he answered, trying to be vague and yet truthful to some extent. He found it a challenge to accept such an action for the luta who had taught him all things good and realized that it was an inherent weakness in lutas like the drain in a washing tub that once the aqua becomes too full of its own pool, the body naturally released the drain cover so that the aqua may not flow out and cause the decimation of the entire subject. Just then he remembered a female's face, Nivian blue, and it caused him so much pain that he left the building before Lez-win could say anything.

It was a familiar face circling in his cerbind like a haunt in the night. She had betrayed him and stolen his love. She, a beautiful Nivian and daughter to a King, had loved another while loving him and when the time came he was discarded, and it was the reason that brought him here – escape. Seranor was his escape though he has yet to know how he reached through the planum barrier, but nonetheless it was the Nivian princess that he felt burning in his body.

She played him like the drum. He had been in love with her, Amana he recalled as her name, and had truly cherished her affection but Amana hit the drum when she needed the music and he sung the tune she wanted to hear until she had found a better drum, a drum that could not be so easily lost and could carry a tune for a long time. Yes, now he remembered Amana with blue tears swelling in his eyes but unable to flow out and release him from this pain. He wiped his eyes when he heard the sounds of Calil and Shev'la returning. They had gone to visit Polinatum for their daily study of elemental worship.

"Anativo, why is it that you hide here?" asked Calil.

"It was not hiding, Calil."

"One day I will teach you a hiding game," he said.

"Hiding game, one day shall be," Anativo said awkwardly as Calil kept on walking to find his mother. "I will find mother," the older brother said to Shev'la.

"Okay, I want to talk to Anativo first," said Shev'la. He had already prepared several times for this moment of talking to Anativo about asking Mareenth to join with him. The courage was not always there and other times he only felt that he was not sincere about the whole thing. Today he was certain and rather than getting into the habit of avoiding it again he decided to go ahead.

"What is it Shev'la?"

"I want to ask Mareenth to join with me," he said straight and to the point.

"Then ask her."

"That simple?"

"That simple."

"Thanks, Anativo." He ran off upstairs to prepare himself.

Chapter 10

SERANOR AND Seragorn glowed poignantly in their
period of black rest. Night was their blanket. And
in their sleepy-eyed spirithood a soft fluorescent
light sprouted from their pores and coated all things
with their undying love. Together, joined as one,
they were both the brightness of the day and the
evening comfort. Emanations colored all parts and
pieces except the few protected by the shadows.
There were always places that could hide from one's
love and the shadows were their sanctuaries.
Flamma reached into the dark glitters of Calil's eyes
and swirled inside their opaque density for fractions
of moments, vibrating endlessly; then in a color shift

the bright of the swirl was refreshed once more. A new reflection of the pretty landscape arose, but still could not hide the sorrow they spoke.

Denial echoed in his head over and over again. His father had denied him the love he deserved and in its place he was given tasks. Everything was a task toward an accomplishment, his father had taught him. Start with a goal, a higher purpose, and work task-by-task until it is done. All things can be done if that is what you believe his father had repeated his whole life. And now those very words were the sharp weapons in his corius. Shev'la has been given, he thought to himself, and why is it that I am left so naked without even the arms of my mother to hold me? An inventor he is; a father he is not. An inventor who cannot stop inventing long enough to appreciate all that he has invented including a seedling who misses a tenderness he can no longer explain.

Calil blankly stared at the gleam coming off of Seranor's hide, drunken with its possibilities and mirroring its shine. He created a dream and saw himself on a futuristic day riding a long-shouldered black *greater talin*; flamma-induced serpentine steeds that glided on arvic waves and designed specifically for Seronian travel. He wore black lutium armor and brandished a long black batier at his side. He moved ferociously, wielding his batier in perfect movements against a gang of morb. Arm by leg by neck by arm, the morb fell in pain and puddles of brown milk coating the land as the warrior spared none and erred not once.

He had been there for some time staring out the window and hadn't noticed Shev'la come in.

"Cal, move a little so I know you're not dead," Shev'la said hoping to cause a stir in his older brother who still hadn't moved. "Life is too great to die now."

"Life has always been good for you," he said dryly without turning his head.

"It has?" Shev'la was busy moving to and fro across the cell.

"Except for you getting sick that one time."

"And almost dying—"

"Do you imagine your body as a statue one day, Shev?"

"I am only happy to be alive. Tomorrow is too far away to predict for me. You know me, Cal, I just move when the air moves."

"But don't you want more? More life? Can our illusion be so distasteful, Shev?"

"It, life, is not so displeasing," Shev'la said, thinking of the luta that he now loved and had decided to marry not noticing so clearly the sadness in Calil's eyes. Calil had grown up expected to do things and not given the same level of attention as was given to his younger brother. "Is it your dream to be a statue?"

"If given the choice, I would not choose to leave as dust. I want to challenge the world and have them remember my name. Calil!—they will yell out. I will be ceramified and my ceramic body will be placed in the hall with the others. The heroes of our planet."

"Life does not last as long as we wish. Father has taught me that. I, for one, do not know what tomorrow will bring. In fact, I feel doubtful that I will ever earn the right of ceramification, and am willing to join the others as dust – assuming that our father does not discover how to keep us all alive forever."

"You won't die for a while," Calil said.

"How can anyone know that?"

"There are reasons for entans not dying when by all rights they should have. There is reason for your still being here as – some say – reasons for us being brothers."

"You're beginning to sound like father," Shev'la said.

Silence.

"Anyway, I found my reason," Shev'la added.

"You have?"

"Her name is Mareenth," he said, unable to hold it in any longer. "I love her and want her to join with me so that we may continue as a pair..."

Calil looked up at his brother walking back and forth across the room looking this way and that. A tear swelled up in his right eye. He could not help thinking about why his life had been neglected so and why Shev'la's only improved.

"Your life only improves...while I am more and more disregarded by father, unseen by mother, and..." Calil's voice shook under emotion.

"...and what? Life doesn't begin the same for everyone. More thought only produces more

mistakes—what were you just thinking about
anyway?"

"Possibilities," said Calil.

"There you go!" replied Shev'la and went on.
"There are always possibilities. Can I give you some
advice? Thinking is good, father loves the idea of
thinking—shat, he's what he is because of it, but not
everyone is like that. Don't think so much."

"It's easy when you have luck on your side," said
Calil.

"Luck is related to the width of your smile, "
Shev'la said, smiling.

"Where did you get that from? Mother?"

"She also could say something like that," he
replied. "I just made it up. If you think about it
you'll agree. The better your life goes, the more you
smile; and the more you smile, the better your life
is."

"You're just too horny over this luta, is that it?"

Shev'la semi-hopped around the cell not able to
stop his enthusiasm. "Yup, I'm hot. Feel the
flamma burn."

"What do you want anyway?'

"What makes you say—" Shev'la was shaking his
side to side in a rocking motion.

"Out with it," said Calil, stopping his eyes on his
younger brother.

"I just have to ask you to do something for me."

"What?"

"Listen to what I'm going to say to Mareenth and
tell me what you think."

"Is that all?"

"Simple..."

Shev'la prepared an entire evening by testing his proposal methods on Calil, who had grown bored of it after the first minute but said nothing to his over-ecstatic brother, before running out in the middle of the dark to find her, knowing that she would be at her residence, as she always was, when Seranor slept.

He considered the timing more perfect than before as he had become strong and radiated health, so much in fact, that he had picked up his aerial acrobatic skills and nearly assumed a natural technique rich in height and execution. From there he took a liking to the lutium *bastion*, curved into a long arc and deadly in its strike; and his interest in the planet grew from the stories that Anativo had told him about Morb, rock beings made from the primordial clay and the essence of Seranivas; and Cerbors, part-rock and part-ceramic beings capable of wielding arvicity. He became excited to know that there was more to life than the life he had.

Anativo explained to the youth some of the memories that had returned to him and described, in exquisite detail, his home planet, Nivata. Both Calil and Shev'la were astounded at the realm of ice and how it was a woven world structured in order and control using numeral physics, mercanomics, technology and politics.

Calil took a particular liking to it. He had believed in what his father researched for hundreds of tios, and if not for the distant relationship with him, might have studied further together; Shev'la had always been closer to his father and so he was left out of their continued partnership. Instead, Calil studied on his own, that was until Anativo grew distant from Tulai and Shev'la. Calil considered it an opportunity and began his step closer to Nivata. From that point he lived, breathed, slept and ate all that his Nivian-come-Seronian had known. Occasionally, Shev'la listened to them talking finding no interest in physics or politics while keeping a sustainable interest in technology.

Numerical physics was the most difficult to comprehend since it was based in the measurement and adjustment of all things physical. This, Tulai thought, was very similar to his discoveries in science and, even he, was an exception rather than a rule. Some of the elder Seronians considered one aspect of mercanomics, the monetary exchange system (MES), as having some role in the town for many had grown bored of such a smooth life and thought that an exchange system where monetary value was exchanged for productive value might pick up the town's morale by creating some kind of game to interact with.

Technology was the easiest to understand as Seranor had hundreds of different technological devices herself. Many of residential devices used in cooking, cleaning and ordering were made of simple but efficient ceramic devices embedded with arvic glyphs to make them functional. Often the glyphs needed to be re-embedded as they faded within a limited amount of use, and an Arvician was found to revive the dead devices. Steady work was found as an Embedder.

Shev'la had been fortunate at his residence since his father had the ability to not only embed, further he could also create new types of devices. Their unamid was filled with many more devices, strange looking and not always the most useful, than the other residences and sometimes were given as gifts when nothing was left to give. Shev'la had taken a deeper interest in communications. Anativo did not speak of communications at all as Nivians naturally communicated to each other using the *diam*, unseen and innate communications grid that connected all of Nivata and which all Nivians had natural access to. From Tulai's observations, the diam existed because of an advanced intellect capable of modifying messages in time and space.

On Seranor, communication was made verbally except when speaking to the elements or the Seranivas who preferred to communicate in twisted songs of verse known to drive many insane if listened to too long and gave others secret powers and abilities if they asked the right questions. Anascal, modified and diluted by the inventor's own recipe, was his favorite drink and he used it to further his arvic abilities often to propel his theories forward. He would drink it during times of great stress from his research. In fact, many Seronians, mostly arvicians, drank a mixture of anascal. It was the drink that maintained a permanent connection between Seranor and Seragorn, and they drank it faithfully and traditionally on a regular basis.

The ubiquitous drink on the planet was anaprimo, the elemental juice. This was drunk practically everyday in minute amounts. Those that wanted to change this habit and stopped drinking for nearly a tio usually got sick, some even died from a sustained disconnection. Excessive intake of either drinks caused degradation, weakening and disorientation. *Sonian* healers believed that a body lost the glue that held them together with the planet's energy for they no longer communicated with it.

Anativo did not have a need nor a desire for either natural drink.

Politics, the art of minimizing society's wills and emphasizing their dreams, was complicated in its theory for politics itself had no structure or form and was the dichotomy of Nivata in the always permanent, and its ability to evolve to suit the needs of the day. Nivian politicians had mastered the art known to them as *adjustification* – knowing when to adjust and by how much. Adjustification, the very act of it went against the entire structure of the planum and its inhabitants who were born in predictable and measurable lives, and also were ruled by adjustification. Politicians gained control by mastering adjustification. It was a late step in what had grown on Seranor as the productization of society, mostly in the bigger urbas. Control, as was commanded by all Nivians, was not made successful by structure, but through the exquisite power hidden in the art of adjustification.

It excited Calil to listen about Nivata. He planned one day to go with Anativo to visit so that he could better understand Nivian power. Shev'la, on the other hand, often dreamt of Mareenth and her shapely body. More recently, he became absorbed by her and preoccupied with how to approach and ask her to join him. Joining was a ritualistic celebration done when a luto and a luta joined their lives with one another. A complete marriage. It was the intertwining of the two that all Seronians felt in their youth. Once joined by a Sagmal, the pair would then produce a seedling who would grow to become the next generation of Seranor. Shev'la had chosen Mareenth to be his partner.

SHEV'LA WAS still running, gasping slightly to reach her residence and all the meanwhile rehearsing the words in his head. When he reached it, he stopped, breathed, and then stood straight up, calm as a tree pointed to the blue clouds above him. He confidently approached the front portal in a measured walk. He waited to be recognized. Soon enough the cell alerted Mareenth of his presence and she opened with a surprised look.

"Shev, what...why are you here?"

"We must meet," he said, confidently.

"Now?"

"Yes—"

"But I can't now," she started but was interrupted.

"Who is at the portal?" asked a luto's voice in the background. Mareenth's face went blush blue.

"Who is that?" Shev'la demanded.

"It's no one...you should go," she said trying to close the portal and hoping that Shev'la would forget this soon enough. But as she tried to close the portal, Shev'la pushed it wide open and entered the cell leaving Mareenth in the background with her hand on the portal and her head down. "You shouldn't have done this, Shev."

Shev'la rounded the hall and reached the empty cell to find the luto who had spoken. It was Romal.

"Evening Shev'la," said Romal in a chipper voice. He was only partially dressed and slightly wet with sweat. His well cropped hair was messed but he didn't seem to be bothered. "I was just thinking about you. What have—"

Shev'la did not wait to listen and in painful anguish left her cell.

"It doesn't mean anything..." she said, making no effect at all as he stormed past her.

Each step away from her cell burned a hole deeper in his chest until the burning caused his face to turn red. By the time that he reached the cora fields on his way back to his residence red tears flowed down his face. He sat and remained there for the entire evening.

By morning, Anativo had come out walking and found Shev'la lying still in the grass. He picked him up and carried him home.

Shev'la awoke some time later that morning. Now on his bed, he last remembered walking in the cora fields. And when he remembered that, the pain in his chest returned; he jumped from his bed obviously angry at his foolishness to believe that he wanted to join with Mareenth the Slut.

He came downstairs and then to the outside in search of his father, he could not find him nor his mother at the residence. Anativo had also disappeared, perhaps he thought, on one of his regular discussions with Polinatum. They had become comfortable together though failed to agree on many points. It was Anativo who had learned the most from him and was deciding whether or not he should commune with the elements. Polinatum suggested that it might help to find out who he really is but Anativo was uncertain as he had grown accustomed to who he had become. The new face made him feel comfortable. He even helped the town to put up new buildings using his knowledge in numerical physics. Tulai's theories continued to develop under his guidance and communication devices became more robust and miniaturized. Anativo soon found that he could easily, if not effortlessly, manipulate arvicity and quickly surpassed Tulai's level of proficiency. He used this to construct things in the town and to develop newly embedded technological devices, *enicoys*, for a variety of purposes. Reanimation became a proficiency with him as he mastered all of Tulai's current theories, as well as modified and improved them with his own ideas.

Anativo stayed close to Shev'la and took interest in his life activities. He could see that his stories had opened doors of new insights in the young luto. It would only be a matter of time, he estimated, that

Shev'la will leave this town to see what he has dreamed in his entan youth. Shev'la learned the fighting style of the arched *bastion*, a weapon that his Nivian friend helped to construct by exciting the ceramic molecules. Anativo found that he learned amazingly fast for a Seronian and was pushed to teach him more advanced moves that could strike multiple opponents with minimal actions, and he had shown him how the custom-made bastion, a curved version of the standard batier, could strike more easily limbs and white flesh after showing Shev'la the details of the Seronian body and where weaknesses were located.

When Shev'la finally told him about Mareenth and Romal after an intense workout, Anativo became angered, not at Shev'la, but at himself for not being aware of the consequences of outside love, and even more fired up for his own weakness on the subject.

"What am I to do?" asked Shev'la. "What am I to do?"

"Nothing. She has mistaken and she will soon enough realize the consequences of her actions," the Nivian said, thinking that after he made clear to Romal his intentions about stopping his ruthless behavior since it would hurt Mareenth and Lez-win. He was going to make it clear until it was absorbed and it did not matter how much effort was required. These actions were going to be punished; he dared not tell that to Shev'la. "Give her some time, decisions are not always made by us. Romal cares for another and she for you." Anativo left.

Chapter 11

SHEV'LA SAT momentarily, his head down with long hair wet with sweat like a shimmering bluish-silver curtain shielding something not wanting to be seen, then went back to his residence to find his mother. Lez-win was collecting some of the goods that had been flashed over and distributing them around to their proper place.

"Mother, can you tell me about love?" he asked, direct and without preparation.

"What is it, Shev?" she asked, slightly bothered by his intrusion.

"Why do lutas love more than one?"

"Because sometimes love is just a word that lutos forget to express," she said, thinking about her and Romal and if what she had done was justified.

"Then why, mother, why do lutas so quickly choose another?"

"Fear...love...she only knows love and without any form of it she will feel empty and will fill that emptiness where it is most accessible," she said this time stopping for several moments with a flamma cleaner in her hands. She thought about Tulai and how she had endured his relentless work habits and how she dreaded it so. Then she thought about Romal, romantic and young, and a warm feeling grew in her belly. "Sometimes she will fill that with real love."

"Then maybe Mareenth doesn't love me."

"She does. She has that sparkle in her eyes when you are near. That confidence that tomorrow everything will be settled," she said, stopping to talk long enough to put away some kitchen items. "But even she cannot wait a whole life."

"But why, mother?" Still trying to get an answer to his original question.

"It is like the—"

"No stories, please. I've heard enough stories from father. Just tell me why, if you know."

"Some lutas cannot wait even for the right love. They fear of loneliness so much that they would rather be occupied with the substituted love of another rather than wait for their true love. It has little relationship to you..."

"Little relationship? It's directly related to me!"

"There is nothing you have wronged."

"And then what will come of this all?" he asked hoping for an answer to sooth his aching chest.

"Love always chooses love," she said succinctly. "Now, allow me to do my duties." Lez-win began to think of Romal and began to miss him and to feel lonely that he was not here to share her life with her. She tried to shut the thoughts out of her head, a weakness fell upon her belly forcing her to sit down crying.

ANATIVO WAS walking in long strides towards the residence of Romal. He did not notice but his feet had not touched the ground for the entire walk and yet his hovering speed was faster than running. Others gasped at the sight of this but remained frozen in disbelief. He arrived, was recognized and began immediately with Romal who came down scantily dressed, abruptly stirred from his peaceful nap.

"You will stop all of your business with Lez-win and Mareenth!" Anativo said clear and to the point. "If you do not stop you will remember this day very well, I promise you!"

"What are you saying? I have done nothing wrong and you are not the judge of my actions whatever they may be," Romal returned in his defense.

"I am judge and jury to what you have done to my friends." Spoken words Anativo never before imagined.

"You are nothing. You do not even belong here. You're just a foreigner. Misappropriated from your own path—" Romal burst out.
"I will say again. You will stop or you will cease to exist!"

"You have no authority here," said Romal. "This is not your planum. I am ruler of myself as all Seronians are! We are the free and you are the frozen. In fact, you are fortunate to be alive."

"I am ruler," he started as he pulled Romal close to him without using his hands and spoke slowly, "to you. And you mustn't forget that." He released Romal and watched him fall to the ground. It felt good to once again wield his power rather than to stifle it. To taste arvic vibes once more. Each moment of extending his power took him closer to who he really was. Romal recomposed himself and cast a spell that would have surprised the best of Arvicians, but Anativo was not of Seranor and without thought dissipated the spell's intentions to suck away his life. He immediately returned a spell, blue-hued and brilliant, that crushed Romal as if a large claw had reached out and closed its fist with Romal in its palm. Anativo smirked then grinned. The hazy eyed luto lover tried to maneuver but was grabbed by the arvic waves and squeezed until milk ran out from all places, then the claw stopped, disappeared and Romal collapsed in a broken pile in his own milk. Upon realizing the consequences of what he had done, Anativo reeled back. Just then, Ossas appeared at the portal opening.

"Romal! Romal!" he yelled upon seeing splattered milk, "What have you done to my seed?"

Others in the streets nearby took notice of the sounds and Anativo became nervous and afraid that he had done something terribly wrong when all he had come here for was to do something right. He thought quickly, then acted. First he threw a cloudy mist in the general area, grabbed Romal's body, then leapt up and flew back to Tulai's chamber under the cloudy guise. The crowd began to quickly shuffle around slightly disoriented. Ossas yelled "Stop him! He killed my seed! Stop him!"

Anativo arrived at the chamber. Tulai had not returned from his meditation with the Seranivas. He wasted no time to recall the reanimation process. After setting Romal's body down gently and stroking his face as if to remind him of the importance of his next set of actions, he stood in the torq of Seranor and began to call Romal's kol. He traced it, called it back and sent up the translucent twisted cord so that it might find its way back to it owner. Being more concerned about retrieving it in any condition superceded all else, so he focused.

Many Seronians had reached Tulai's residence and even Tulai himself had returned, surprised to find so many here. They told him that Anativo had "killed and stolen Romal's body" among other more murderous talk. Tulai became worried at the endless possibilities to what he had brought upon this town and his friends and had to find the truth. Ossas was angered beyond the point of reason saying, "Prove to me that my seed lives. Unless

Romal is brought out alive in reasonable time, Anativo will die!" Ossas was an Arvician of sorts himself. Several others in the gathering crowd agreed.

"He shouldn't have been awakened," Ossas continued, "it is your fault Tulai that my seed has died, if that is what I saw. You are responsible!" yelled Ossas pointing his finger at Tulai who had no concept of what was going on.

"But I have done not what you say and, furthermore, perhaps your seed is not dead. Can you confirm that he did indeed die?" Tulai said hoping that if what he thought was correct and Anativo had returned him to the chamber to save him it would be entirely possible that Romal will not have died and had been reanimated.

"He was limp in the Nivian's arms."

"Then you do not know if he is dead and may have jumped to conclusions far faster than they indeed happened," Tuali said unexpectedly.

"Tuali, you are protecting him!" someone yelled from the back of the group.

"I am not protecting him," started the inventor, "but we should not claim a luto dead unless they are truly dead. I have studied the ways of death half my adult life and death is not as certain as we have believed."

"Then bring him out and we shall all see!" said Ossas slightly calmer than from before. "Bring out my seed so that I may see what has happened to him."

"Bring him out indeed and we shall all see, just let me go inside and I shall return soon enough with truth. Patience will provide an answer," Tulai said as he entered the chamber to find Anativo and what he had done. He secured the entrance after reassuring the others.

Anativo was sitting down in the center of the torq with Romal's body an arm's length to his right. He, a Nivian, was crying and he did not know why. Tulai approached him. A pile of small, crystals had formed beneath his face.

"What happened here, Anativo?"

"I killed a Seronian," he started, "I killed...and I could not accept what I had done and so I brought him back...It wasn't difficult...he had to come back, so I had to after killing him...then I healed his cracked body and...it is wrong what I have done?...I feel it so even though I was not meant to feel. This world, this planet strikes me deeply in ways I cannot prevent..."

"No one must know that you killed him," said Tulai afraid of what would happen when the risk he brought to Ulaq was found guilty of murder. He himself would be sent out and his family would fall farther in ruin, deep into the recesses of his personal affliction. "—but pray tell me, is he all right?"

"All right. He is all right, once again."

"Romal," Tulai said looking at his sleeping body, "Romal, wake up. You have been sleeping." The body stirred, opened its eyes and awoke.

"Who calls for me?" Romal asked in a groggy state.

"It's Tulai. Do you remember what happened to you?"

"I have no memory. I was napping at my house then Anativo was at my residence...Why am I here?"

"Anativo brought you here after you collapsed at your residence," said Tulai knowing it was a lie but realizing that it would prevent further trouble. Disastrous trouble. "How do you feel?"

"Tired...but fine. Where is Lezzy?"

"Who?"

"Lezzy, where is she? I must find her."

"First, let's go outside. There are many ceramin worried about you including your father." Romal went home with Ossas. The remainder laughed off the whole incident as nothing but a dire attempt to cause attention for the royal family. Lez-win had hidden behind Yutillo, an extremely tall luto with long black hair and who worked in the center facilitating the delivery of items to all those who demanded them; and she did not come out until Romal's back was to her. Yutillo was born with extraordinary cerbal processing ability, twice that of a normal luto, as well as gifted eyesight. She was relieved, wiping tears from her eyes as she watched Romal return and not being able to be with him at this moment. Tulai approached her. She did not notice immediately.

"All is fine," her husband said.

"What happened?" she asked as the remainder of the ceramin scattered back to their residences disappointed at what they had seen. Within a minute, all was quiet at the gate of the chamber, not even Anativo was around.

"He is all right," he said, looking for a reaction on her face. Nothing was made apparent. Even if it were, Tulai was no expert at reading faces. "I do not know the details of what happened. Only to know that when he came back he first spoke of you."

"What do you mean?" she asked, feeling some confirmation to the love Romal shared with her. And now she was beginning to accept that she also shared with him.

"I must go back to the chamber to speak with Anativo," he said. Tulai silently turned around without another word with just enough time to catch the momentary shift of her eyes; his cerbind could not rest knowing what Romal had said.

Time had crossed paths with occurrence and she knew that she must confess to Tulai out of simple respect for what he was and not for what he wasn't.

"Tulai, wait." She reached out her right arm with an open hand.

He stopped. "What is it?" he asked though he already knew that Lez·win and Romal had grown together. It was the sense of her touch from her long smooth fingers, or the roughness in their brushing, that made it clear. And he felt that he, from his excessively focused life, was responsible but no more responsible that she was for not communicating this to him from the start.

"Tulai, I'm sorry."

"Sorry, for not telling me?" he asked, his back still to her and his head down, but now his theory was confirmed.

"I'm sorry that this has happened. I did not intend it to happen," she said taking one step closer then hesitating before taking another.

"But it has happened."

"Yes."

"And you made it happen, Lez...and maybe even I made it happen..."

"...we haven't been the same, Tulai. I have not been happy for more scores of tios than I can remember while you have indulged in all things that made you feel comfortable and happy."

"What is it you want from me?" he asked hoping to find an easy solution to the pain in his body if it were possible.

"I love him and wish to be with him."

"And what about Calil and Shev'la?"

"They have grown enough to understand."

"Maybe. I will let *you* explain it to them."

"Are you angry with me?" she asked as guilt surfaced from inside.

"When I was a youth it was easy to be angered by such things. As a creator, anger is an energetic distraction. So, am I angry? No. Am I perfect? Also, no. Am I feeling the sadness of loss? Yes."

"I don't mean to hurt you, Tulai. I have and will continue to love you but our love is that of tender compassion and not of nubile passion."

"If you do not mean to hurt me then why is it that you work in such secret ways?"

"I do not know."

"But you have done so."

"It was not a plan. It just happened."

"Lez, rain just happens. Having an affair doesn't just happen."

"Well—"

"Your reasons of infidelity are displeasing me more. Maybe it is better that you stop."

"I want to explain...but there is no explanation. It happened and...and that is that."

"It happened..."

"Yes—I love him, Tulai."

"And our love—my love, what of that?" he asked.

She tried to push the words out but they would not form themselves. She could see her husband retracting himself, closing himself off like times of intense experimentation, and it confirmed the correctness of her choice. "Tulai—" she finally blurted out. "Please don't shut everyone out."

"If you truly love Romal, I will not stop you, Lez, but you will understand if I do not support it." Tulai walked away from his silent wife. He now felt an emptiness inside as if he had spent time in the nilospace. Love was around and nearby and not inside.

He accepted Lez-win's decision that day and turned his attention away from the love of others to the love of his dedication to research that would one day save Seranor and all those who lived here.

The next two months became entirely dedicated to his work. He was driven, like the days of his youth, to find something not previously seen. If he could not mend his relationship with Lez-win then he would find something else that he could indeed mend. Love, unfortunately, had no solution. There was no theory to solve and without theory there was no basis from which to work. He was determined to solve some unsolvable problem and did not stop until a discovery was made.

Chapter 12

TULAI CAME running towards the chamber, angry
and worried, his hair messed and a with a few
night's sleep missing in his dull eyes. He ran inside
and upon finding Anativo, stopped dead in his
tracks. Months of intense research were evident in
his dilapidated grooming.

"Anativo," he started, huffing and puffing from a
short sprint, "the theory...there's
something...something..."

Anativo already knew what he was going to say,
he had sensed something wrong when he reanimated
Romal. But he became preoccupied with the missing
love in his life. Each time he thought about it the
spike pushed itself deeper and the beautiful female

in his dream laughed at him. In his then excited state over Romal's reanimation he skipped over the theoretical insufficiency as unrelated information and the very mention of it now weakened his knees.

"The theory is cracked," he quickly finished Tulai's sentence for him. "I had analyzed it in-depth…" he sat down on the table, threw his hair back using both hands and then dropped his head with full hands covering his face. "How could—"

"I didn't see it before," said Tulai.

"What were we supposed to see exactly?"

"The form changes after death. The kol changes."

"Yes, the form…"

"It wasn't clear until the Seranivas had told me that in the nilospace the kol believes its host is dead so changes its form to exist solely in the nilospace so that it may prepare for its circulation…it is this that I failed to see," explained an exasperated Tulai holding back his torment of failure. "When I reanimated your body and retrieved your kol, your body had not died and so its—"

"Its form remained the same," added Anativo.

"The same," Tulai repeated.

"And so we assumed that this factor was not relevant—"

"But it is not only relevant – it's crucial. Unless the kol can accept the possibility of being reunited with its host then—"

"Then it will try everything to get back to the nilospace including—"

"Including leaving the host abruptly, no matter how strong it is, powerless against it for the kol makes decisions."

Tulai did not speak, only paused briefly.

"I must tend," the curious inventor started again, "to this new factor. It must be solved or the entire theory and our body of work is useless if the kol will not remain in its host. Let us work together to solve it. I will need you to help me to study the nilospace further," said Tulai. He knew that traveling the nilospace would require Anativo's ability to remain untouched by the unpleasantness of it. He could also periodically travel but could only confirm ideas thoroughly tested by his partner. Nivians were more resistant to the supernatural effects of the nilospace.

"Certainly," he paused for a long moment. "Tulai, you understand love more than I have been able to," Anativo said, shifting to the buried topic in his cerbind. "What is it to feel love? It is one thing that I do not remember so clearly."

He laughed. "Love? What do I know about love?"

"Each day I exist here I take one further step away from love rather than one step into it."

"Feeling love is not a choice. It is just there and if you are open to it you can feel it. Sometimes you feel warm and secure and though you cannot see love it is there shielding you from the world outside."

"What does it feel like when you were in love with your wife?"

"She and I...we've changed..."

Anativo paused. "What *did* it feel like?"

"It is not an easy topic for me, friend. When I think about it I feel pain...discomfort...and...anger. Yes, anger. Complete and utter agitation, if not for the beauty and the...fullness it gave me. Love is...well, our first and best connection, I think."

Anativo attempted to find consensus with his friend's definition and his own ideas to finish the theory on love, but nothing matched.

"Come," Tulai said. "We must find an answer to finish the Anativical Theorem. There will be plenty of chance still to talk about love in the future."

They spent many late evenings in the chamber trying to reconstruct the old theory of reanimation with a patch to connect the critical point between stability and instability. Anativo would often venture into the nilospace to understand it better as he was able to endure the terrain much longer than Tulai who on occasion would go to confirm new information.

The more time Anativo spent there the more comfortable he became with it. Months passed and each week Anativo's character altered and then degraded.

He would do strange things. He built a residence for Poy, the father of a close friend of Calil, then an hour later he decimated it, all with a wave of his arms and a brimming smile. Arvic manipulation turned to an obsession as he commanded destructive spells and beat the planet's ground with it often examining the damage he was capable of; and all the while the satisfying smirk on his face. The other town members feared him more and more, and when they could they avoided him or cut him short in conversation before he said something to insult his previous friends. Anativo would often seem lost in thought or looking at an empty spot as if there was indeed something there. Soon enough, comfort turned to addiction and Anativo would find himself hiding in the nilospace when he chose to, when he couldn't bear the thought of what was dear to him anymore.

Tulai finally traveled to the nilospace – the place of transformation – after expending his thoughts on the theorem without definite success then went on a fact-finding excursion and found something that left his milk dry in his veins. A piece of Anativo's kol remained in the nilospace while Anativo was still on Seranor. This, he had not seen before. Anativo had traveled so frequently that a piece of him had grown accustomed to being there and he could see more clearly the reasons why Anativo's character had changed; had become far worse than before; far more greedy; more desperate for the things he wished for; and delved more often in arvic manipulation designed to destroy rather than build. Tulai had to be careful how to handle this considering Anativo's ability to know most everything and his current behavior.

Several days after this new discovery, Anativo came into the chamber, his skin emanated an icy cold air around it. He was expressionless, not the same as when Tulai had found him. His skin had grown a deeper blue shade reflecting an icy scale in the light.

"You have hidden something from me," said Anativo, unfriendly and short.

"No..."

"My necklace and rings."

"I was wondering if you would ever take them back since you have become more of a Seronian than a Nivian."

"I can only be what I am."

"That is not true as you are aware of."

"I am Nivian and Nivian is what I am. Now, I ask for my things a second time."

Tulai walked a few steps, waved his hand and in the near wall a small portal appeared. He opened it and pulled out a ring and a black necklace. Both had the mark of the Nivian King Llinduus. Then he placed them carefully, as if admiring their beauty, on the table top. Anativo walked over and picked up the necklace with the kium square then placed it around his neck, once there the necklace clasped itself into a seamless chain. He lightly grabbed the black center piece covering the blue spike. A blue glow in the shape of a spike sprang from it and encased Anativo's body. He closed his eyes and immediately after a dull blue arvic shield surrounded him. Tulai, by now, had stepped back several steps and had prepared his exit for something that could have happened but didn't. Anativo was lifted off of his feet ten centimeters from the ground and his body shook violently for several minutes. A massive surge of arvicity flowed throughout the chamber and had activated some still devices on the shelves. Tulai had to run to shut some of them down. Minutes later the translucent blue spike surrounding the Nivian stopped and he dropped to his knees in a loud thud that shook the ground. Tulai stood several meters away watching, hoping that neither Calil nor Shev'la should come to witness this and any other of Anativo's changes, but over the last period Calil had become so attached to the strange friend, and Tulai so distanced, that for some, time may have been permanently lost. Finally, Anativo gave out a loud cry of anger and pain combined, that sounded for several seconds longer than any Seronian could muster even on the best day.

"Remember me for I am here!" cried the Nivian then he arched his back while still on his knees. "I hold my arms and all is clear! Remember me for I am here!" he cried out again this time crossing both arms across his over-sized chest. Anativo spoke these lines and repeated the movements several times before finally rising. He raised his head and now his eyes had gone translucent orange.

"Anativo, what has happened? What has happened?" asked Tulai, concerned for his friend.

"Rebirth!" the Nivian yelled out. "Now, I will take Seca."

Tulai, upon hearing the utterance of the ancient relic, moved to guard the vault but Anativo's force was impassable and he was pushed away. The reborn Nivian carefully removed the ancient silver rod, handled it as a familiar piece, and left the chamber laughing and ignoring Tulai, who stood motionless and worried.

He could not help to think that satisfying his theories and the life of his seedling, his plans had been so convoluted. It was then that fear entered his body. It was then that he realized that he was alone and now his two seeds were in danger and he was powerless to alter the course of nature again, and yet he wasn't willing to accept this unreasonable resolution Seranor had given him. A plan began to brew in his cerbind. The Nivian black ring with embedded crystals, the ring all members of Nivata wore, remained in his keeping.

That evening Tulai could not sleep for several hours, afraid to accept that he caused the pain of his loneliness; and that he delivered a Nivian to the planum of entans. He did eventually fall asleep many hours into the night and dreamt of his beautiful wife Lez-win. She reminded him about love and the first time they had met. He was attracted by her beauty and kindness as he couldn't resist the temptation to walk over to the long white-haired luta with red sparkling eyes. She had stood there outside in the rain, wet as if she had just taken a river's bath. An irresistible wind propelled him from behind and he couldn't stop floating to the sparkling beauty.

"Attraction," he said, waking in the middle of the night. "Attraction!"

It was in the rhythm of attraction where all beings connected, he quickly deduced. That was it! I have found it. Attraction creates connection; and connection remains constant. It was irresistible. We must find a way to attract the kol back. Attract it and we remove the choice to return. And what attracts a kol? Another kol. A desired kol. We must find that which the kol loves and show it that that love remains, once back in the body it will have forgotten that it had left and with health restored all will have been safely put together. Reconnection complete. There is still time for protecting Romal. Anativo must stay out of this for he has gone too far and I fear that it may be too late though I must try to prevent disaster. If I can solve the problem of the kol then I can save them both. Anativo is my friend. My responsibility. "Work raises its demands once again," he muttered to himself.

Chapter 13

THIRST FOR life, the desire to drink one's own milk as if to quench oneself in one's own passion, grew strongly in Anativo (in his case it was not milk but naqui that burned on his lips). For arvicians and arvicerers there was only one path to progression and it was found in the tussle of exploration and experimentation. All spell casters, shapers of arvicity, could only increase their manipulative ability through its very process. Arvicity was an ocean of energy whose total weight could both crush and swallow whole those who tried to control it. But it was the path of the arvic shapers to warp rivers and streams and pools to gain access to greater arvic force. It was also why there were very few great arvicians on the planet. The Nivian's innate advantage over an entan's was obvious. Anativo played with the ubiquitous element like aqua tossed back and forth in a seedling's hands. In no time at all, he bored with such complacency and chose to play with danger in its substitution.

He experimented with advanced albeit dangerous arvic spells attempting to embed them into round lutium devices which would then be thrown at objects and once the command verse was sounded, the ball would release its embedded spell usually destroying what was around it in a radius effect. He had attempted to embed a gamma glyph, a flamma command that disintegrated objects in its area of effect, into black lutium but failed because of the lutium's inability to keep such volatile levels of arvicity for very long, and before he had released it far from his hand, it had set off turning an entire five meter radius into a gamma sphere that obliterated everything in its range and, if Anativo hadn't protected himself with his own high level lists, would have annihilated him; instead it vaporized his entire left arm, shoulder and rib cage searing his blue face black on one side. It did not kill him. Most things on this planet could not in fact kill him and if it hadn't been his own spell that fumbled he would have likely remained untouched and unharmed. He became infuriated at the common materials that he was left to use and swore to create his own in the days to arrive.

He healed after using spells, potions and salves but could not remove the blackness left on his face. He returned to his tricks this time colder and more distant. He no longer found time to speak to Shev'la and so the young luto spent more time with Mareenth, and at the sight of this Anativo only confirmed in his corrupt cerbind of what life had done to him. The Nivian renewed his strength and began to use arvicity to shape ceramic and found a way to animate lutium which even Tulai did not understand. After weeks of experiments he molded several pieces of lutium together into the shape of his missing body parts with a two-pronged piece on the end of the arm to be used for handling simple things. He then embedded glyphs, new arvic spells that he created, into the arm and by way of arvicity attached the arm to the side of his chest cavity. It held and gave him limited mobility on a temporary basis, needing to be re-energized every few days.

He traveled to the Nivata mountains staying weeks at a time and each time he returned his length of stay in Ulaq became shorter and shorter. Calil would occasionally travel with him to the snow mountains as did others.

Anativo called a meeting for all the inhabitants to join in on. Only him and Calil came to lead the groups. Many wondered why. To some it was quite obvious. Anativo's vision needed larger numbers of followers. It was the oratic draft. The first meeting left the audience astounded at the augmented power Blue Skin had. Never far from his grasp, Seca did not play a part in the demonstration when Anativo

warped arvicity to decimate and reconstruct objects
of various sizes. When the Nivian encased the
building where they all stood in ice, it was enough to
convince even the most stubborn of entans, which
were few and difficult to find. One hundred
followers joined and left to train in oratic spell lists
and ways. More drafting sessions followed and
membership grew to six hundred after three months.
Calil would lead them into the icy mountains for
weeks of intensive training. Ice and frozen
temperatures deeply affected the porcelan structure
and milk of entans. Some could not endure the
pains of this level of extreme physicality and were
killed as they tried to return. Control left no
options. They called themselves the Timor of Ice,
striking fear in the young, with their renamed
leader, Zorath. When Zorath's fledgling recruits
returned they only caused havoc and aggravation
among the remaining peaceful Seronians. Soon the
town members were happy of their leave and
dreaded their return.

Calil led many smaller excursions to raid deep
caverns and to attack urbas not far from Ulaq. Each
time that he returned his skin turned a deeper shade
of gray and his abilities multiplied along with his
manner of weaponry.

After the last leave, Zorath, Calil and a
contingency of fifty returned from Nivata mountain.
Calil proudly wore black-plated armor with a kium
black rader at his hip. His long hair flowed in the
wind. He had become his dream. Adventure ran in
his veins, milky white was only its color. The

Nivian, dressed in a one-piece suit of flexible blue ice that did not melt, carried no weapon for his arvic abilities had grown a hundred-fold since his discovery and were doubling in power every month.

Tulai and Polinatum knew this well from their commune with Seranivas and the elements; they could find rancidity in their attempts to stop him. Calil had not changed, he had become another as if his kol was swapped. He only listened to his Nivian leader and not to his family or friends. In all of this, the elements reassured the Sagmal that what had happened was expected and that nature always provided the balance. "Emptiness will be given fullness; and fullness will be given emptiness," they had said.

Shev'la, after seeing the discouragement in his father's eyes, went to the residence Zorath had built. His need to know overweighed his fear of the situation. The followers respected the about-to-be married entan, mostly from Zorath's respect to his father, and did allow his trespassing. Upon entering the cell in which his old friend lay he felt the deep cold chill in the air and saw his breath a cool white mist in front of him. Several armed guards maintained watch. They too seemed lifeless. The Nivian sat in a large, tall-backed blue chair, sitting like he ruled the planet that he was on. He swallowed whole shards of fresh ice from a nearby container.

"So, you have finally come," said Zorath, crunching away at his last shard.

"I have," replied Shev'la.

"Tell me young Shev'la, what has been the greatest lesson in your life."

He waited a moment examining what had become of his once friend. "All things have reason. Even you—"

"Even you, Shev'la. What will you achieve in your life from such a limited body? You have known of these limitations, have you not?"

"That which is in my dream."

"Ahh, the dreams that come and go in a night's wind. Perhaps your dream is already gone and you are all that is left from that dream. Then what will you achieve?"

He paused to think. "New dreams."

The Nivian laughed loudly. "Just like your father—idealistic."

"To be like him would truly be a great achievement. He has contributed to society in ways none could ever achieve, and even revived a dying Nivian whom I once called my friend."

"He only used my power to fuel his inventions. He never cared for me as he led himself to believe."

"He loved you—"

"Never! Never did he love me."

"He did and it is why you are here. Love is more than the word you want to hear."

"No, Shev'la. It is why you are here. Your father never told you about how he came to save your life, did he? All the potions you took – which he took credit for – were taken from my body. I healed you. I saved you. Without me you would have died long ago."

An absorbing memory entered Shev'la's head. He tried to assimilate before a response found its own way out. "Without me, you would have never been found...So our lives are intertwined more than you have let yourself to believe. We are all equal fools of fate."

He laughed loudly again. "Fools are those who wait. You have waited your whole life." He continued to laugh. "Calil!—Your brother no longer waits. He grows stronger and more capable." The fully armored Calil flashed to a spot beside the Nivian king. "He has excelled faster than you. Care to test his abilities." Calil stepped forward after the Nivian waved his finger.

"Anativo—" Shev'la began.

"Anativo—Anativo is dead," said Calil, interjecting.

"He is right. I am Nahkli-Li Zorath, great Nivian of Nivata and soon to rule all of Seranor," said the former Anativo. He had discovered his true self.

"You were once my dream," said Shev'la, disappointed at what life had provided for him.

"Your father will soon be a dream also."

Shev'la drew his bastion. "Do not speak of my father like that!" Calil drew his quattro-bladed rader. Shev'la knew that Calil was under complete control of Zorath who by now had corrupted his every fiber. He did not want to fight his brother.

"Come Shev, let us match up once again. I have lived my desires and not hid in them like yourself and the others. I am well prepared now. Come..." said Calil.

"You will fight soon enough brother, but not with me. I am not your enemy. Your enemy sits in front of you hiding in politic. In his one of many masks does he so hide."

"Again you delay and prove me right," said Zorath.

"I do not delay. You would have me battle with my brother to feed your corrupted kol. You can never understand love and I can no longer share it with you. As for you Calil, Seranor still loves you and always will. Remember that because to forget it will be your end." Shev'la quietly backed away into the darkness of the corridor and peacefully left. None followed.

DRUMS ROARED throughout the town signaling the joining of two Seronians. It was a special day for Shev'la and Mareenth, not one that had come easily. Shev'la, beaten and disturbed from his failed attempts to grab the attention of the one he loved, all of a sudden stopped chasing. He had been playing her game and under her rules he was losing every round of the match. A dove that he chased through the cora fields taught him a valuable lesson as it flirted away from him faster and faster the more he pursued it. He eventually caught it, using his aerial techniques, and found that he lost interest in his prize and had no choice but to let it go. The bird happily flew away. Shev'la, on the other hand, smiled as if bright flamma erupted over his head.

"Chase and all will be chased away," he said to himself. "Interest and all will be interested."

From that very next day, he stopped chasing Mareenth, stopped calling her name, stopped thinking about her, though deep inside he did not stop loving her. As he stopped his thinking, it became increasingly easier to think of other things and so he did often courting other lutas, casually, of course. He met Laqua, a shapely luta with short white hair down to her ears, and her wide smile and sparkling gums. She reminded him of his mother. They spent time together on a casual basis all the meanwhile he would have his eyes out for Mareenth and what she was doing. Mareenth, it was rumored, was asking friends about what Shev'la was doing and who he was with. She began to stare his dates up and down if ever they met in the town center. She even became angry with Shev'la for no apparent reason.

Shev'la took this as a positive sign that his ploy had worked successfully enough for him to now draw in his little prey. He arranged it so that Mareenth would be at the eaden at the roughly the same time he would be there to see some friends. They met, argued, kissed and in the middle of the eaden, Shev'la asked her to join him. Her eyes glistened with red tears and she accepted.

On their marriage day, Mareenth wore specially made white cora silks embroidered with brown lutium shells that echoed the drum sounds. Beside her, Shev'la wore a full green cora silk suit fitted with a white sash at his waist that flowed in the breeze. Many of the town members came, some said that they had seen Anativo briefly but if he came he did not stay for very long. The joining ritual was filled with soothing drum sounds that cheered the whole town for the day and they all rejoiced in diluted anaprimo and the fruits of Seranor. His father and mother were both present. He came alone. She with Romal. They were independently happy for him. Happier than normal since losing Calil to Anativo.

His mother and Romal were comfortable together. She came dressed in luxuriously pressed whites while her wealthy luto companion walked in a full length body suit made of a swirling red pattern. Lez·win and Romal were also to be married after Shev'la. The excitement from his own wedding drowned the confusion he felt about his mother, and seeing her facial smile he noted that she hadn't smiled for some time; he loved her too much not to be happy for her. Lutas, he thought, may take a lifetime to properly understand, and then this idea fitted him and he looked forward to his peaceful tios later in life.

Shev'la's father was ragged and inattentive. He visited his seed before leaving early.

"Father, I am so happy that you have come today," said Shev'la.

"You are my seed and will always be my seed. It doesn't matter where the wind blows you," said Tulai.

"Mother is happy..."

Something distracted Tulai in the sky, but when Shev'la looked there was nothing. "Father, are you okay? I worry about you."

Tulai massaged his hands trying to find a way to speak what he wanted and unable to find the necessary thrust. Anativo troubled him. The Nivian was migrating to the path of ora. His arvic skills multiplied exponentially and was putting fear into the local ceramin who had not been fooled by his verse. Other Arvicians would surely feel his presence in the global arvic pool. They would know of the wrongs that had been done. But Shev'la still wasn't aware of something that the inventor's kol refused to divulge. Tulai struggled with it hopelessly.

"I'm fine, Shev. Things are changing and…it may continue in ways that I cannot predict…I hope…I…" Tulai rested both hands on Shev'la's shoulders.

"Father, do you want to tell me something?" he looked into his glistening eyes.

"Many things, seed. Many."

"What is it father?"

"I—"

"It's okay…"

"I, you must know someth—"

"Shev! There you are!" cried Mareenth as she ran up to the two of them, her wonderful scent trailed behind. A brightly brimming smile was posted on her face. "I've been wanting to find my new husband and…oh, hello, Tulai. I am so filled with joy by your presence here today."

Tulai nodded and worked a smile. "I must go, Shev. I·I·I have to finish something that must be finished soon..." Tulai pulled himself away.

"Father?"

"Bye, Tulai!—He'll be back," said Mareenth. "Come on, I want you to..."

NEARLY SEVEN months later and many sleepless nights, Tulai had completed a series of new identification, tracking and connection spells that could be used in the nilospace to find that which the kol most deeply loved and using it to attract it into its original place. This would ensure safety in the reanimation process and was the missing link that they had overlooked. His cerbind had grown increasingly preoccupied with Anativo and his deteriorated state, of which he had not paid attention to during his intense spell research and development.

It was a long time that Tulai had spent refining the Anativical Theorem using all that he had learned and even longer since he remembered his friend. Zorath had become a story of telling in Ulaq's bars. There was rarely a week that went by that something didn't happen. A couple of months ago, Anativo sucked out the energy of a healthy arvic pool and turned it black by the time he finished his selfish deed. Shortly after that, Julao, an Arvatist, tapped into this pool accidentally, it polluted his veins and he died a black corpse. The Nivian couldn't be blamed for Julao's own inexperience but the ceramin were not comfortable with it.

Calil focused on fighting. He learned to fight hand-to-hand combat and tested his talent for shedding milk on other young adventurous types. As his skills improved his opponents were left with more grievous wounds. Some died. Lutos grew fearful of Calil as he was the right hand of the blue-faced foreigner. They blamed Tulai for detriments they all faced.

Most ceramin were relieved when Zorath and Calil ventured into the mountains. Only then, did comfort come to the town members, but there was an angry group growing. Tulai would not listen and could not do anything. He was not capable of undoing what he had done. Reanimation worked in only one direction and it couldn't be canceled so easily. With the Nivian's current level of power, none could match him.

Zorath's arvic presence brought Amid Levin once again. This time he did not come with his seed but with three lutium-plated warriors with the signs of House Levin on their breastplates. Amid held meetings with the town *wisans*, the old and wise lutos such as Polinatum. They talked in many meetings and decisions still eluded them. Seronians were not fighters by birth, not like Nivians who learned warring skills from an early age. House Levin was special in this respect. It was responsible for developing weaponry and minor technological items, as well as armor. Could one House go against Zorath? Amid hoped that Tulai could provide some inspiration to their dilemma but the inventor was so absorbed with his studies that he had little to offer. More importantly, Tulai needed to see his old friend. The one who he revived from a dying state after stealing his powers for his own selfish purpose.

Tulai finally drew up the courage with which to approach Zorath. Tulai had gone to the residence that the Nivian had built only three kilometers from his place. He approached it steadily. Inside him grew the levels of guilt for waiting this long. When he arrived at the grounds he could see the icy residence, triangular in nature, quiet as if no one lived in it. He was allowed in without an ounce of resistance as if Zorath's hand showed him the way and went to the front portal, within seconds the portal of translucent material opened. He entered and in a large rectangular cell he found the former Anativo, wearing cora silks beneath blue-tinged armor covering his torso and right arm, his left white arm covered only by the red silky material. Nothing covered his blackened, grotesque face.

"You have come to kill me?" Zorath said at once.

"Kill you? Why would I consider something so ludicrous? You were my friend once, Zorath. Do you remember this?"

Zorath swallowed a large ball of green snow. "War will soon be at hand!" said Zorath looking at his old friend. Tulai did not speak. "I let no one come here except my best fighters and most loyal such as Calil. You have come to talk, have you?" he said holding up his goblet. "You are in time to share in my fresh brew of anascal. I made it myself with an extra special ingredient designed to get you more."

"We must talk plainly," said Tulai.

"Of course, it has been 53 tios since you have found me. That I shall not forget."

"I fear you have injured yourself and I am to blame," Tulai started, "it is your kol I worry about. It has made you sick with greed and corrupt with power."

"Sick and corrupt. Do I look sick to you?" Zorath asked, raising his head.

"Yes," replied Tulai, looking at the vile being that was once a beautiful Nivian and now a deformed monster bent on causing pain on others for the pain he had inside.

"I am at my peak, my mountain of life. I have grown in ability and can wield arvic spells that would destroy others, including yourself. I am sick! You see a sick Nivian here?! We Nivians are born to win while Seronians seem born only to exist—"

"Anativo—"

"Do not call me Anativo for it is not my real name. I am Zorath, a once great Nivian who would be king destined to rule, betrayed by those he once trusted and loved, and he who shall rule regardless..."

"An—Zorath, you must listen..."

"Since my return, I have always listened but *now* they will listen to me. And they do."

"Please, one last time—"

"Talk before I lose my patience."

"Your kol is partially trapped in the nilospace. I have seen it," said Tulai.

"The nilospace is part of me now," Zorath replied. "We are happy together."

"It draws strength from you and corrupts you for it cares no longer that you live or die."

"Nonsense! You cannot accept that I have grown more powerful than you. You speak nonsense. You only have theories, I have the real and you yearn for what I have! You yearn!—I do not."

"You must retrieve your kol, I cannot—you must. If you don't, I fear it may soon transform you in ways even I cannot imagine."

Zorath was looking at his prosthetic left arm, opening and closing the pincers at the end of it. "Too late!" He dropped the arm down and the pincers cut through the end piece of the lutium table. Tulai remained calm but in his cerbind had already prepared his escape with arvic spells ready to aid him. "Too late. You talk as if I'm dying when I am at the highest vitality I can remember. You yearn for what I have," he said picking up the broken table piece with his right hand then melting it in his palm and shaping it into a long black dagger, then stabbing it hard into the table top still holding onto the hilt. "Leave and yearn elsewhere, Tulai, for I may soon forget the goodness you have given, and you may never yearn again. None of this town will yearn again. This planet needs me. Just like you, it yearns for me," Zorath said, shifting his voice deeper and more serious in tone as he spoke.

Tulai felt the volatility in his old friend's voice and the danger arising from his unstable presence. He left knowing that time had already marked the future of his latest project; he had misjudged his previous conclusions at all levels it seemed and now could only ponder at the possibilities.

With the fourth perfection, Zorath could claim Seranor for himself and forever enslave all Seronians as none could stand against his power when fully realized. Zorath had stood temporarily motionless after the one who found and saved him from his death exited the portal. Then, suddenly, he released the dagger and went to another cell at the back. When his long tunic finally cleared the table top and ran smoothly over the dagger's hilt, a molded face of a beautiful Nivian female, Amana, tearing from the left eye was cast upon the back of the hilt.

Chapter 14

WALKING HOME, Tulai wandered aimlessly through the town not able to put sure thoughts to what had happened nor what would happen. He felt an increasing need to leave Ulaq, certain that Zorath would only release his dementia upon those closest to him. But the danger was too high to warn all the members. Zorath would be sure to find out and slaughter them all before they stepped into the next region. Seca was far too powerful to defend against especially in the hands of a Nivian. He was trying to think of a more peaceful solution to an imminent reality. Amid had already asked him several times to attend their secret meetings. He had refused,

insisting that he needed to meet with Zorath first,
and it left him without position.

About an hour into his troubling stroll, he had
somehow ended up at Lez-win's new residence where
she now lived with Romal; signs of weaknesses in
Romal's body had not yet shown themselves. Based
on his new predictions, time would come soon
enough he feared, and to complicate the situation,
they were planning to have a seed. He sat, tired
from his walk and news of Zorath who was becoming
what his friend Polinatum had warned him about
from the very start, even Lez-win suggested against
it, and all the while Tulai did not listen thinking
that they could not understand the essence of his
quest, his contribution to the protection of Seranor.
His blindness had seen clearly.

Hours passed quietly in the still of the night and
he wondered what to do next seeing that his theories
had cost him all that he loved and now his only
comfort was the cold, dry verse in his manuscripts
and his broken devices strewn about here and there.
Was life so worthless? He chose not to answer that
question in his current state of cerbind.

Tulai fell asleep there on the cool green grass and
dreamed of traveling in the nilospace chasing
Shev'la whose kol was stolen from him by a cloaked
figure. He moved quickly to reach the crying sounds
of his seed's kol. By time he was able to retrieve it,
Shev'la's kol had ceased to exist; and feeling
completely overwhelmed for what Tulai himself had
done, he nearly exploded in a fit of tears and loud
crying as if he hadn't cried for an entire life. Still his

seed was dead and no amount of crying was going to bring him back.

He opened his dripping eyes to a loud crying behind him. Quickly wiping himself while turning his head he noticed that the sound was not only coming from Lez-win's new residence – it was the sound of Lez-win herself. Without thought he jumped to the emergency and ran to the unamid as quick as quick could be, flashing part of the way. He waved his hand and flew to the front ajar portal. He ran inside to the cell the sound emanated from. Lez-win was hunched in the corner of the far wall. Romal, or what once was Romal, lay sprawled in the center of cell. There was milk everywhere even on the ceiling and splashed across all the walls front to back, and left to right. Lez-win's clothes were soaked with it.

He stepped closer trying to understand what had happened. Romal's body, desiccated and hollow, lay quiet except for short breaths from what lungs remained. Then the breathing altogether stopped. The room fell silent.

He looked over to Lez-win then around then to Lez-win. "Lez, have you been injured?" he asked, completely calm in tone.

She kept crying in the corner.

"Lez!" he yelled. "It's Tulai!" She finally moved her head up then briefly turned to look behind her not believing it at first. Upon confirming that it was indeed Tulai, her first love, she pushed her fat chest up, and struggled away from him. Tulai was several steps ahead of her and arrived to help her stand on her wobbly legs before she fell over. Lez-win was several months pregnant.

"Don't touch me!" she cried. "Get away!"

"It's me Lez. It's okay."

"Don't touch me," she said in profuse tears and helplessly collapsed into his arms.

"Are you hurt?" he asked again now more worried since he hadn't known that she was pregnant.

The crying continued for several antagonizing minutes. "Did you see him?" she asked, streaking her tears from the brush of hair and hand.

"Who did it, Lez? Who killed Romal?"

"Who killed Romal? You killed him, Tulai!" she started crying again. "You took him from me...you saved the planet...dead...everything is dead...everything..."

"Lez, listen to me...Lez," he said trying to take her out of her fits of anger and depression. "Listen!" He grabbed both arms pulled them straight and shook her violently; it hurt him to do this but he had to know about the seed, he had to know when she and Romal had mated. Was it before or after Romal's reanimation?

"Lez, Lez, listen please...when did you get pregnant?" he asked still holding her arms, her head looking down and she was trying to sit down but Tulai would not allow it.

"The father is dead," she said tossing her head left and right.

"Did you get pregnant before or after the incident?"

"Before or after," she repeated. "Before or after—it's still a disaster."

"Before or after?" he said with a firm voice and pulled her closer to him trying to get her face to look up. He tried to block her natural scent from entering his pores but could not. "Lez, it's important."

"It's important, everything to you is important," she said finally looking up at him, red tears on her face and speaking more slowly to make her point. "Everything but those around you."

He knew that she was right and it was only now that Tulai recognized his innate weakness. His inability to see the finer details in life and quickly wondered how much of this would be passed on to Calil or Shev'la. His eyes swelled red.

"I have mistaken—you knew that before we joined. I have been sorry for weeks that I cannot remember. Sorry for what I did not consciously do and yet have been incriminated for," he said to her face and this time she did not drop her head. "All that I loved yesterday has been taken from me and it is I who have taken from myself. I have been my own obstacle to my life. All for the glory of Seranor—"

"The glory of you."

"Yes, maybe...maybe it was for the glory of me. And now my selfishness has started a revolution in all things, and has put me here for a reason to hold you one last time."

She stopped crying and collected her thoughts pulling her arms from Tulai who had released the tension of his grip.

"Anativo has become another...Romal...oh, Romal...and you, Lez," he said, "you were once the flamma in my chambered life. Please tell me that you are okay..."

"I—"

Her body lurched forward into Tulai's arms but it was not her force that did so. Tulai grabbed her tight as her body convulsed violently again and again in repetition.

"Tulai! Tulai!" she screamed. He did not know what to do but knew that he could no longer hang on to her without hurting her so let go, stepped back, and manipulated an arvic spell only he knew as he suspected that the nilospace was involved. Lez-win's body fell hard to the ground.

Tulai's spell shown, bright and illuminated, a faint but connected cord from her chest into the nilospace. The seed's kol wanted to return and didn't care whether the host agreed or not. Another spell tried to attract the kol back which calmed it temporarily and gave Lez-win a chance to speak. Tulai tried to prepare another but Lez-win's soft voice distracted him and he moved closer to listen. He had missed so much until this point.

"I am at end," she whispered as if unsure the time that remained. "Do not return me to this place, I ask that of you..." Her voice was drowned by the wail of kol and body being torn apart. The kol inside her chest became desperate to get out and in a burst, that even Tulai's spell failed to counteract though he tried valiantly, freed itself then latched onto the cord and returned. Only a moment later, another kol, that of Lez·win, removed itself as its body perished in a heap. Tulai watched it, not able to breathe or blink, until it scaled its own cord back to its origin and vanished. Knowing that she did not want to return.

Tulai stood there for many minutes shocked at what he had been responsible for and shamed at his failure to prevent this from happening.

When he told Ossas to follow him to find Romal, the effects of those findings reverberated throughout the town until every member demanded that Tulai be removed as should Zorath. Tulai became responsible for getting Zorath out though knew clearly that Zorath would not leave nor could he have any power to make him do so. So he considered his options. He understood what Zorath wanted. He wanted power as all Nivians did. The source of all ora on Seranor came from Seragorn, enslaved from long ago and intertwined in the planet. I cannot stop Zorath, he thought. But maybe Shev'la still can. He had drunk Zorath's naqui and lived. There was no telling what new path was open to him now but it was tied to the blue stranger on Seranor. Chances were the one thing that couldn't be fully removed.

SERANOR GLOWED, casting light shadows on all that walked upon her hide, while she slept another peaceful night and revitalized her realm in preparation for what was to come. On the hilltop next to a cora tree whose twisted trunk had grown thick shaping itself like a Serag, the failed Nexatist rested. The Serags were long serpentine beasts, descendants of Seragons from long ago, born with legs to walk the planet and to keep all things in transformation. They were large and deadly in battle when provoked and sitting under this tree, Tulai could gather a sense of their protection; he felt safe and distant from all the trouble his life had assumed.

He thought to himself, one step in one direction can lead you ten steps on the wrong path. Only one step was enough to start the process and I have taken several more than necessary. All reasons would reveal themselves soon enough, but until then I must ensure that my seedlings, whom Lez-win has unwillingly charged me with, will live on and have good enough chance to mark the histories of tomorrow with their name, and in my dying moments that I may know that what I am about to do will start another step that may one day put everything that I have wronged back onto the right path. He leaned back onto the trunk and felt its warmth enter his body. He sighed. "Seranor, I have not forgotten you but in my haste to prove one thing I missed the beauty you already possess. I have lost all things I did not see before...I have lost my Lez-win," Tulai said out loud for the Seranivas and the elements to hear. He remained under the comfort of the tree and soon fell asleep.

A call of his name awoke him several hours later. When his eyes cleared of the fog he looked up to see Shev'la smiling at him and saw the reflection of himself; it reassured him that all his life was not wasted and encouraged him to continue with additional fervor. He reached up his arm to touch Shev'la and felt the strength in his body; his seed had grown into a luto and though he would always be Tulai's seed soon enough Shev'la would carry his own responsibilities and make his own steps.

"Shev, come here," he said as he pulled on the beige cora sleeve on his right arm.

"Yes, father." He knelt down beside him.

"Know this, that wherever we may fall in our lives, know that I love you and always will."

"I know that father. I know for I love you."

"Then listen to me now. Danger grows in this town for us."

"From where? Zorath?"

"From all places, Shev." He sat back and prepared a spell.

"What are you doing father?"

"I will cast a spell to protect you."

"Protect me from what?"

"From things that can hurt you." Tulai feared telling his seed of the true purpose of his spell. The energy required to manipulate the rich arvicity was draining and he almost fumbled it twice. The spell came out wrapping itself around Shev'la and then became absorbed into his body where it would start its slow germination. His seed didn't feel anything different and wouldn't for some time.

"My corius feels better but my hunger has gotten the best of me. Let us feast on a morning of food," said Tulai.

"Fresh clay is always a pleasure."

As Tulai rose to his feet to return to the residence, he felt a wave of arvicity ripple across the terrain passing through his skin and stimulating all that was inside. Shev'la felt only a subdued effect. Tulai faced the arvic wave to taste its power. It numbed his body if only for several moments.

TWO MAJESTIC mountains of ice like twins in the twilight stood erect as if guarding the Versos. The mountains, ten thousand meters tall and half as wide, of Nivata emulated pure cold, all things designed to freeze; to subdue the very life of the planet. The ice came to enslave Seranor. It came to reduce her will and the center of the planet remained frozen for ten thousand tios before entans came. It wasn't strange that Zorath had returned to his source of power. And where he stood, he was a spec in a sea of greenish snow.

He had been there for several days contemplating, regenerating his desires to what he was now to do. I have come so far, he thought. I have traveled between worlds and yet my travel was not done. I am displeased at what I have been given and have been put in a prison of the worst design. This planet was the failure of the Versos for all things that exist here were temporary and trapped in a world of pain and sorrow. I have been saved not by Seranor but I have been saved by myself. Those that have betrayed will in their time be betrayed and those that have been given misfortune such as all of Seronians and their flaccid beliefs shall be eradicated, and shall serve me in my ascension to the throne of Nivata and then to the cosmos. No longer will I thirst for what can never be caught. Love is an infection, a disease to weaken the intention of beings. And I have been infected to the point of my own extinction, but will no longer need the taste for love. All that has been loved is now a forgotten memory thrown to the blizzard and frozen for lifetimes yet to come. Let the others feel the disease and let it keep weak all the kols of Seranor. I will now make claim to what has always been inside – the truth. I will awaken all those who can serve my purpose to extract the power of Seranor and Seragorn. This planet which I thought was a prison was actually a gift given to me to serve the true purpose of the Versos for ora was the glue that bound all of us and would glue together the impermanent fragments of the cosmos. Seranor fears my power already, this was true, and now all of her seedlings will know that fear.

Standing in the chasm between two ice mountains, Zorath rejuvenated his power. Twenty meters to all sides of him rose a hemisphere. Inside he threw his arms calling the ancient pool of arvicity deep inside the planet that until now none had succeeded to tap. Brilliant blue it came and he spun it on his hands like cora silk in the hands of the best weaver. The arvicity ran through him, it danced with him and he relished in its stimulation and power. His arvic powers had grown and now surpassed all on Seranor, not even the greatest Arvicians could defeat him alone.

The Nivian arvicerer warped the gate between life and death calling to the ice to produce what he searched for. His calling penetrated far into the ground. Slowly a black-blue pool of glacial aqua extracted itself from the ground and began to form into that of a large misshapen body. Several minutes later a creature of ice completed itself. Four meters in height, it stood on two legs, body of plates thicker than the thickest armor and a pointed head such as Nivata mountain herself. Its oversized arms moved with sounds of ice-cold blocks being shifted together. And the smell. There was no other smell like it. A putrid stench that could stifle the smell of nature's purest ocean, and could only come from the beast of Seranor - Malkar. These monstrous beings were neither living nor dead but were the vile byproduct of the elements and knew only to create waste and to prevent changes from occurring on the planet's surface. Malkar were the ancient enemies of the Serag and often disguised themselves so they could travel the land without notice. Their power to disguise was often limited not only in length of time but more so because of their moody and unpredictable personalities. Vileness could only be disguised for so long.

The ice monster roared in its birth. It had no mouth, just a large, razor sharp and jagged opening. It took notice of Zorath, cast out both arms springing forth a frosty liquid from his fingerless fists. The black liquid hit the very spot that Zorath stood but not before Zorath cast his spell flashing him to a point directly beside the small mountain. The beast spun itself into a blizzard beating hard against the Nivian who only laughed at its futile attempts and did not notice that his left arm had been completely shattered from the gripping temperatures. Finally, Zorath waved his right hand and the malkar was stopped and forced to reform on two legs. He closed his fist and the ice began to melt and the monster screeched in pain. It tried to fight but was no match for Zorath.

"Yield or perish!" said the Nivian avoiding the use of too many complex words. Malkar spoke a limited vocabulary though could understand most levels of verse.

"Not yield," replied the Malkar.

Zorath deepened his attack and the Malkar's body began to shrink as it melted. "Yield or perish!"

"Not perish," replied the beast in crude verse.

"Serve me until I release you."

"Not serve," said the monster and it motioned to attack.

"Serve me until I release you or until your death!" Zorath's fingers rotated slightly and loud breaks in the monster's body were heard. A chunk of its body fell off and the monster screeched.

"Serve and pollute."

"Yes. To serve and pollute."

"Pollute planet."

"Speak your name, monster, vile beast of ora."

"Raskavron."

"Then Raskavron," he started then relaxed his hand and the pain stopped, "come with me. I am Zorath and we have a Seronian town to dispose of and decimate."

"Raskavron will serve."

Chapter 15

AN HOUR and a half washed away in the delight and
pleasure of the freshest clay in Ulaq. Each piece was
sliced raw at the source near the outskirts of the
town, and an invigorating soup of white clay
cleansed their palates and their inner workings. The
tired inventor sat with his younger seed on the porch
of the unamid. A breeze, sharp and short, blew their
cora clothing in spurts of anger, fluttering the cloth
like the hand of a rabid morb. Above, the ruffled bed
sheet of blue clouds were dull and moved ever so
slowly as they were pulled across the planet.

It will still very early and only some of the town
had awoken and were in the center practicing their
painting or having group discussion to invigorate

their cerbus. Tulai recalled his own youth spent
learning the way of entans much as he still did now
though more worn in his ways and without the smile
he once had. He even painted; choosing to give his
works away to the loveliest luta he could find on that
day saying that she *inspired* him to paint such art;
but he never lost his love of creation nor his passion
for the things he believed and it was more a part of
him now than in his lost youth where all things
meant everything and nothing at the same time.

He held his left hand out near his face feeling the
wind passing through his fingers quietly gazing at
its wonder and thinking about the arvic ripple that
he had felt in the early morning. Powerful levels of
arvicity had been used and it was near to the town,
not more than three or four days walk, he thought.
He looked once again at his seedling, his only friend
and family. Lez-win had died, Calil had failed him,
his theories had opened the wrong doors, but
Shev'la—why have I done this to him? I must
explain more to him. There was reason to all things
on Seranor.

In the windy breeze, Shev'la could feel that the
air around his father had slowed and was conjuring
something from deep inside. Perhaps his own
perception had made such things noticeable.

"Did I ever tell you about how Seragorn and
Seranor became the planet?" said Tulai, then
lowered his arm and turned his head to Shev'la.

"You have told us before," the newly married
entan started. Mareenth was busy in the large town
square and wouldn't return for a couple of hours.

His marriage had made him docile and conservative. "You told us that Seranor chose to become the planet and then bore Seragorn to keep her company."

"Seranor did not choose. She was tricked and enslaved."

"But she is the source of life—"

"And even the most powerful can be subdued, made a slave as she was; and she was betrayed by those that were the seeds of her seeds."

"What has happened, father? You have been strange this last period. I, too, am unbalanced by my mother's leave but I have seen the smile back in her eyes that she could no longer find with you."

"Your mother is another story, Shev," started the inventor. "She is dead, died last night after Romal."

"Dead—And you do not tell me!"

"I tell you now, Shev."

"Now—"

"Yes. It was a terrible, terrible thing...if only she had told me of her pregnancy I might have been able to...such terrible things are happening..."

"You killed her!"

"No, I—"

"Your selfishness killed her!"

"Shev'la Khan, you speak too far!"

"My mother is dead and it is your hand that has touched her life, as it was with Romal and Zorath."

"Your father has made many mistakes but he has not killed what he loved. My hand was not in her death."

"How did she arrive at her death?"

"She became pregnant with Romal's seed after he had returned...he was not stable, I told Anativo...Zorath...none would listen..."

"Your theories were responsible."

"Your mother was never happy with me. I don't know why she endured it for so long. My theory...unfinished theory that I did not cast...all my work lost..."

Shev'la fell silent for a long time.

"Mother was dying in our residence from the beginning. She could never escape you and your ways," said the young luto.

"We all choose our own lives whether we are conscious of our choice or completely unaware." Tulai had made choices by not making them and this reality hurt him. Indirectly, he ignited the whole series of events which were taking away his family and his ceramin.

"And now her choosing is done. She is gone."

"You do not know my love for your mother. I have never shared it with you in fear of losing what was left."

"But you never showed her love."

"You are young and you will see that love changes as all things change. Fail to see that and you will live in pain. It is something that you cannot keep. Love is the master of illusion."

Shev'la cried silently. He could not stop the red tears from falling. He only controlled the sound.

"There is another tale yet to tell and I believe that since it was me who started it that we should all know it more clearly. I fear, as you have seen, that

Anativo, who now calls himself by his true name Zorath; I fear that having found the rod he will eventually find the other pieces."

"There is more to this rod?"

"Much more," Tulai answered, still uncertain whether or not to continue.

"How much more?" asked Shev'la and his father could no longer resist the pressure.

"This is one of seven pieces capable of mass destruction if given to the wrong hands as I fear it has been given, and once the set has been made complete it will cause a shift. An arvic shift that can erase the planet and all its inhabitants.

"In the time of old when greater beings than you or I ruled the land, many items of destruction and transformation were constructed. Some were suits of armor impervious to elements, others were rings that enhanced arvic manipulation and unbreakable weapons, but this piece that Zorath now holds is part of a seven piece set that enslaved both cosmic Seragons: Seranor and Seragorn. The piece cannot be destroyed for it rules creation and supercedes all except what we have yet to see. This is a piece of the Arvinstrum, seven devices designed to control the life and death of Seragons, long serpentine and scaly creatures capable of tremendous elemental energy and transformation, and the original inhabitants of planet Aquanomicus.

"But the Nivators, avian beasts of destruction sent by the Nivians on the twenty-third planum Nivatasek, wanted to rule Aquanomicus and hoped one day to extinguish the brightness of planum

Mettadi·di Flamma and freeze the entire versos so it
could warp a new cosmos. Our home planet, known
because of its original oblong shape made of pure
aqua, became the battle grounds.

"All five Seragons were captured, tricked by the
beauty and charm of the Nivators and held in
Nivata, the Nivian kingdom. It was during that
time that the Nivators began to freeze Aquanomicus
into a sphere of ice. The Seragons: Seruumr,
Seryntr, Seraal, and Serng; under the leadership of
the female known as Seranor, escaped Nivata from
those who sought to destroy them, and again arrived
on Aquanomicus to do battle to stop the Nivators.
Half of Aquanomicus, starting from its core and
outer center, was already frozen and the other half,
encircling the ice, remained as aqua and all battled
from the great depths of its spherical ocean to the
cloud·filled skies. After time unknown and
immeasurable, the Seragons conquered the Nivators
and forever banished them from their plane.

"Some of the Nivators charmed and had offspring
with Seragons who were later able to stay behind
and survive. Most of the offspring, Seraniva, were
eventually killed but nine Seranivas were enslaved
and transformed into spirits to serve the Seragons
and to help them tend to the planet's needs. But the
Seraniva spirits later tricked the Seragons and
enslaved the five leaders, sealing four of their spirits
in Periodic Ice. The leader Seranor, powerful in all
elemental energy, was made the cosmic Seragon and
was forced to bind the sphere with its body for the

liquid planet had become unstable and volatile from all the battles in its deep icy ocean.

"Seranor's body was forced throughout the oceans of the half planet and the other four seragon's lives were spared and made eternal. It's serpentine-like body, once in a state of a slow death, absorbed much of the aqua and filled out the sphere. Then its body surfaced and created mountains from its back and created chasms from its outstretched limbs. The other four were bound and sealed and then made into the four elements of ceramico, cora, flamma and arvano.

"Ancient weapons from the battles between Kozotal and Nivian were created, used, hidden and some were lost on the planet. These included weapons of mass destruction, as well as those of creation and transformation.

"The four elements then created the atmosphere and nature and all things necessary for life from Seranor's body. Then the Seraniva spirits created the non-beings, Morb, from their essence and the primordial ceramic of the land to entertain them.

"Time passed and Seranor had grown tired of binding the planet and tired of being alone only to serve the Seraniva and Morb. Seranor became jealous. The planet started to shake and crack as Seranor gave birth to a seed, Seragorn, before it finally began dying. Seragorn, hidden by the four elements, escaped from detection and began to move throughout Seranor's body, eating its way until it stretched three thousand kilometers.

"The Morb were innately more powerful, so the Entans learned to manipulate Seranor's primordial energy and also to master the elemental forces and to become them as needed though these last abilities have largely been forgotten save a few who live dedicated lives. As the entans grew in power, hastened by drinking spirit potions and learning the secrets of arvic energy, they began to win against the morb and so the Seraniva gifted some of the morb with intelligence and arvic abilities, Cerbors, and sent them to search for Seragorn to try to stop her from helping the entans.

"Still Seragorn was not found until several entans who found, made, and drank the mixture of anaprimo, the drug of elemental meditation, and betrayed the elements by telling the Seranivas about Seragorn and where he hid. At once, a search was made and Seragorn was found intertwined throughout the land and sea. The Seranivas gave the secrets to a seven-piece set of arvic energy magnifiers and devices, the Arvinstrum; constructed long ago by the Kozotal, that would be used once Seragorn was caught.

"Before she could escape, cerbors and Ventans, gray entans corrupted by arvic power, wielding high levels of arvicity traced nine *artus* points on Seragorn's body and locked its joints into position. There were immense changes in the land's surface as Seragorn, along with some entans, resisted and fought. Thus began the period of the *Cerborian Repulsion* which lasted a few thousand tios. In the end, Seragorn was bound to where he lay last."

"What is it that the Arvinstrum can do? Why are there seven pieces?" asked Shev'la, previously captivated by the story of the planet's creation. "How did Zorath come to possess one of them? Why did you say nothing before?"

"Each piece has a specific function," Tulai started again. "One will cut the planet's hide, one to dig, one to wash away the clay, one to suspend life, one to protect, one to release the Seragon, and one to prevent the cosmic serpent's life from disappearing from exposure to the non-cosmic environment.

"Her head was unearthed using the Arvinstrum and her immense energy cycle was injected into Seranor, so that all the energy was distributed throughout the land and therefore shared by all arvatists, of entan and morb variety. Seranor was reborn as a slave. And, in turn, the cerbors and ventans quenched Seragorn's anger, for what they had done to Seranor and him, with the energy of Seranor which it, in turn, recycled into nature and kept life eternal. Seragorn was now able to constantly transform itself and always remain the same so as to not disturb the newly formed planet and its inhabitants, but sometimes Seragorn still moves and causes changes in the land when it is reminded of what was done to its mother.

"The Arvinstrum was constructed by the Kozotal using the richest flamma. The pieces were later hidden and some protected though no one knows what has happened to them anymore, probably strewn about the planet."

"Expose the seragon? To what end, father?"

"The planet's core source of energy. Pure arvicity that can be manipulated if controlled."

"Only a Kozotal or a Nivian could…"

"Now you see the danger, my seed. In a Nivian's hands, the Versos would be laid bare and could be reshaped. Especially with the primal rhythm of Seranor and Seragorn."

"So Zorath will find the Arvinstrum for this purpose?"

"I am certain that he will eventually try. There is one other device that he would need and, if I am correct in my knowledge, he would be unable to open the case that protects it."

"Why is that?"

"He is of ora though I suspect he is not aware of this fact in his lustful rape of supremacy. The object could not be known to him. None have spoken of the device since its creation."

"How do you know of it?"

"From my sacrifices, Shev. From my sacrifices."

"Zorath will most certainly find the case."

"Perhaps."

"Where is the case?"

"Lost. Nowhere. I do not know."

"How would such a thing be lost?"

"A special case – called Seranor's Box – was created by the Kozotal Yerrotian Kel-pa and stolen by her brother. Even the Kozotalians have problems. It has been said, at least I have heard repeated more than once by those of the wise and able, that it corrupted his brother in a temporal pool of all things."

"What is the device, father?"

"The case holds the *Orbis* – key to the Versos. One who has the Orbis holds the cosmic key. The builder of life. A cosmic repository. It is without doubt that Zorath will find all seven pieces of the Arvinstrum but he cannot find the cosmic ball so easily for it is hidden in a case no mortal has ever seen or heard for more than 8,000 tios. This box is said to be made small and square with the figure of a Seragon fixed prominently on top like a handle to the lid. None could mistake it when seen."

"If he finds the Arvinstrum, then—"

"Then we are doomed to die. He will find them, but he must not find the Orbis."

"Who will stop him?"

"You must find the orbis."

"Me? But father—"

"Hear me, Shev'la Khan. You must find it and put it somewhere safe."

"But I have just joined with Mareenth and will bear a seed. I am at my most comfort in all my life..."

"There are no others I can rely nor trust."

"Father, what could I do to protect this orbis that would prevent Zorath from getting it?"

"I am not sure but surely there is something." Tulai paused in thought. "There is little information on the composition of this orbis and how it was made. Maybe you could release its powers and thereby stop Zorath..."

"You are to say to destroy it?"

"It would prevent Zorath from using it."

"Father, look at me clearly, please." Shev'la grabbed Tulai by his chin, gently. Tulai could see the youthful joviality that he had given him. Shev's hair blew wildly in the wind and that caused Tulai to smile. "What power do I have against a Nivian? I am just a seed, a seed in the wind."

Tulai's smile remained as he spoke: "You have been spared for reasons I do not know and that you must find. You must find that reason. Can you understand that, Shev? Find the reason and we have a chance to correct the wrongs that have been made."

"Mother is dead, Calil is corrupted, and Zorath...he is changed. Maybe what is true father is that I am just another Seronian destined to live a life of peace and tranquility."

"When Zorath cracks open the land and sucks out Seragorn's energy there will be no more tranquility, no more peace, no more planet for they – these things – bind the planet. As you and I are bound to her."

"Then perhaps I am the fool, as Zorath once told me, and will wait for the end," Shev'la said. He felt feint and sick from all that he had just learned. He was losing all that he loved and was given the greatest of tasks to save Seranor, from a father who had caused her demise. His father had put all of them on this path. "It is because of you that we are all like this. Mother is dead, in case you have forgotten. She is dead! Do you also want me to die?"

"No."

"You save Seranor!"

"I—"

"You are killing her. You save her!"

Shev'la stormed off in a rush.

"It is not in my ability to achieve such things...anymore," he said to himself. "Not in my ability...and if not in yours we will perish. You are the one who is capable. Oh Seranor, forgive me for what I have done. I have meant only right and now all is wrong...there is a strength in Shev'la, I know it. Show him that strength at any cost. He is all that is capable..."

Chapter 16

AMID LEVIN called a final secret meeting to rid the planet of the Nivian Zorath. His followers numbered nearly a thousand, but most were still in the early phases of training. There had been several deaths recently and everyday town members grew afraid of dying for a reason they could not justify. Average Seronians were not born warriors. If anything, they followed the three cornerstones of thought and were prone to creating artworks, discussing philosophy in the square or simply using flamma to keep them entertained. Seronian thoughts were considered to be highly evolved and the ultimate stage of planetary beings. The fight had been fought out of them thousands of tios ago when their enemies were abolished or abandoned. Only the morb and cerbor remained but they kept to themselves in the mountains or forests, and would attack if and when provoked. These ugly creatures had become somewhat fearful of entans themselves.

"Fear has been swept off Seranor for a hundred-hundred tios," Amid said to the council of six in a sparsely filled chamber with only one source of flamma. "One being can drop that emotion? One against many? How this is so, I cannot find ways to properly imagine." Harsh shadows formed on his face from the singular light source highlighting the anger of his disappointments.

"He is not one being. Zorath is a Nivian with unlimited arvic power," answered Yano, a wisan and an arvician wearing yellow cora silks and a translucent choker necklace.

"But he is alone. Will not Seronians rise up against him?"

"Why do you want this war, Amid? It will be a horrible war that we bring upon ourselves. Zorath has not done anything to demonstrate the seriousness of his intensions—"

"He is a Nivian! Would he show it to your eye so that you may know it clearly? We may resist a fight because we have a choice. Later there will be no choice and many of our ceramin will die."

"And his power is most succinct."

"He is weak," Amid answered. "He is weak in power when compared to when he regains his full abilities."

"How do you know this?" asked Yano.

"I have measured the density of the arvicity that flows through him: His arvic weight, fellow wisans. Nivians have greater capacity for arvicity because their body is largely composed of stable ice. It is in frigidity that arvicity flows less encumbered. Kium, we know, is the best conductor. Weapons of kium become superconductors of arvicity and are most dangerous on this planet.

"When Zorath first came to our planet something prevented his arvic conduction. It is still not fully functioning and I also do not know what it is. I do know that his body now conducts arvicity with little resistance. His kium items only super-enhance his innate power. So, I repeat. We must stop him now before his power is at full."

"He already outmatches us. How would we even attempt it?"

"We combine our talents in feromentan," said Amid.

A round of muttering and whispered questions followed.

"This technique has not been tried for several thousand tios—" said one wisan.

"In practice it has worked. Feromentan will multiply all our abilities several-fold if we can join three of us together. I suggest myself, Polinatum and Yano."

"And not Tulai?"

"Not Tulai. He is not fit to go against the one he raised. Tulai would cause great danger to us."

"I believe Amid is a trusted companion of Seranor," said Polinatum. "His family history speaks volumes against the morb invaders. It will be a risk but life is not made in safety. I will join you, Amid."

"Thank you. And you, Yano?"

"Polinatum is the source of inspiration for all of us here. There is no need to ask."

"Good," said Amid. "Let us prepare before Zorath reforms from his latest excursion. He must be made irrevocably dead and we must be wary of the silver rod in his hands."

"I will summon help from a Serag," said Polinatum.

"Then do so, dear friend, for Seranor is more dear than all our lives together," said Amid. The room fell dark and a brief shuffling of feet ensued before turning silent once again. Not even an arvic trace remained.

DISTANCE HAD grown between what was once Tulai's seed; a kind, desperate luto that could never attain the attention he believed he deserved, and time, filled with tension and despair, entered his corius and gave him a new dream; a dream of death and rebirth into the numbed body empty of feelings. Calil and his father Tulai no longer talked to each other, not even Tulai spoke of him anymore for the mere mention of his name brought tears to his eyes, dark red tears that stung his smooth white skin. Father and seed had become distanced beyond repair and Zorath was there as his hatred, death and pain – absolute corruption.

Zorath had reached a point of assuming what he once was – unforgiving, unrelenting and incapable of feeling – only this time he had even become a more powerful arvicerer than ever before and this was due to Tulai, father to his loyal warrior. As each day drew to a close, Calil, corrupted with an internal fire that could not be extinguished, moved closer to the cold realm for it brought him a soothing touch; he shut off all feelings except those designed to control, and became servant to a Nivian who would one day be king of Seranor. But trouble had grown since Zorath knew that only Tulai, he who had assisted in his rebirth, had the power with which to destroy him; he knew his weaknesses.

Zorath was not able to control his own addiction to the nilospace and traveled without preparation to the quietness within. Each return to Seranor removed another measurement of density in his body and slowly he was becoming a dual-space being. At the rate of his digression, which he could no longer adjust as Tulai originally warned him about, his body would soon enough become a non-body; and he, a non-being. There was nothing for him to consider. He believed that this would make him unstoppable on the planet. He planned to construct the greatest servants to walk the land in his name and to control the entire planet. But first he had to remove the traces of his past so that none could follow nor stop him. For this he was to use Calil. Despite all that he was or not was he could never directly annihilate the one who acted as his father.

Calil was commanded to see him in his make-shift cell. He came immediately, mentally and physically prepared to take any mission so requested from his would-be king. Raskavron stood coldly to Zorath's right side. Seca, silver and smooth, lay upon the table in front of the Nivian. All the cells had been frozen, but the cold temperatures did not bother even Calil, his white breath that could be seen in the dim light revealed his mortality.

"Lord Zorath."

"Calil, welcome."

"How may I serve you, my Lord?"

"Tell me Calil, what is the weakness of Seranor?"

"Love, Lord Zorath. As you have taught me. It weakens the mortal fibers of all beings created on Seranor and it is why this planet will soon enough surrender to the might of Nivata."

"And how will these beings surrender to our might?"

"Love makes them weak and soft. Our Nivian kingdom will annihilate them all then we shall form a new planet, a planet of structure and all things permanent."

"Before this happens, Calil, we must remove those who can oppose us for they have secrets against us."

"Then they shall be annihilated."

"Yes, they shall and I want you to do it. You must kill Tulai. He is gifted with far too much knowledge of us and is the only one who can hurt us."

"He has hurt many, my Lord."

"Now, he must die for the pain he has given."

"He will feel this pain."

Calil fixed his rader firmly in its scabbard, turned in military fashion and left the cell heading towards his father's residence.

"He has served his small purpose sufficiently enough. If he fails or not, we now prepare for our action." Zorath twirled Seca in his right hand. "The town must be wiped clean from the surface. Nothing shall live! Nothing shall be remembered of this town except for a giant hole! And I trust you to do your part, Raskavron, or I will end all your days with but a single note," he said, stopping to twirl the long rod and pointing at the malkar. "Now, follow Calil and kill him when it is time. Burn him in ice."

"Burn in ice!" Raskavron started laughing, deeply and loudly. "Ice will burn!" He started walking toward the exit. "Ice will burn!"

Zorath laughed, slow, deep and certain of his glory.

DEVICES, TOOLS, manuscripts, and a host of miscellaneous items were scattered across the once organized chamber. At the back of the wall, Tulai crouched over removing some of the more valuable manuscripts that he had prepared, some that had never been used, yet. He moved in haste knowing that not everything could come with him but wanting the most important items to follow where he went. In the morning he had told Shev'la of the danger of Zorath and it did not take much to convince him. Shev'la also knew that Zorath had been corrupted by his own greed for power and hastened by his fear of what he could not understand – love. He only had to convince Mareenth who had grown accustomed to the comfort of the town away from the life she once knew. She did not see the danger as father and seedling said, and more to the point, she did not care for anything that Zorath was involved with.

He was only a misguided beast in her opinion who never let love into his corius. This was far from the truth since Zorath was a Nivian, a being of the greatest arvic powers, who had made his way to planet Seranor, a place where no single being – not even the Serag – could match his intelligence, strength, or arvic manipulation. He had spent the entire week trying to explain this to Mareenth, the luta he loved dearly, who constantly refused to accept what it was that he was saying. New ways were found to convince her and shot down all the same.

From her view, her life had already been lived from before when she was a prostitute in Casus and now Shev'la wanted to take her back to the same city she had left and this she could not accept. She had escaped her old life for reasons of survival and was unwilling to return to the place that had become her past.

"Why choose Casus?" she asked.

"Father believes that his influence there could make the necessary changes," said Khan trying to convince his own cerbind of the need for such a shift.

Mareenth pondered in a heavy breath. "I cannot return to that place," she replied.

"Why?" asked Khan but she had already started walking away before he even asked and he was left without an answer.

Casus was both a deadly but opportunistic urba where all things could be found and made possible. Adventurers from all over Seranor flocked to the urba in search of fame, some in search of fortune, and all in search of power. She cared for none of those things only to bear a seed or two and raise them to be good members of Seranor. Shev'la also wanted this but there was more in his corius than even he knew. Life as a simple luto with simple dreams could never satisfy the giant hole in his kol that could only be filled by achieving far more than he realized that he could. Occasionally, he felt this emptiness and it gave him grander visions of his life, but within moments he quenched its thirst with the love of his wife, the future mother of his seedling.

Time shortened and after his father told him in the morning of the next day that they must leave by nightfall in fear of all perishing together from the hand of Zorath, Shev'la once again tried to talk to Mareenth. His father chose Casus since he wanted to further spread his knowledge to help ceramin and the urba was the most pliable for new ideas.

She was in the top floor of their quiet residence overlooking the mountains; she had been staring out the window all day in the direction of Casus, thinking about what life had turned into and if her decision was made proper by staying here. She indeed loved Shev'la more than she had ever loved another and most loved him for his ability to accept things without question or heavy demand. A simple luto really. What had been occurring over the past week was indeed strange since her husband never pushed her for anything, and it was perhaps that she had grown accustomed to not being given any demands that she had refused to accept that they had to leave the town she also had come to love.

Mareenth returned to the bed with a painting of Shev'la after the Aquatic Competition. He had won the competition to swim under aqua over the greatest distance without surfacing. None were able to match his endurance or capacity to remain under and when he finally surfaced more than half a kilometer ahead of the best he did so with such enthusiasm and vigor that even he could not control. He jumped out from the river running at full toward the crowd that had gathered. It was that focus in his eyes and the uncontrollable expression on his face that convinced her that he wanted more and was capable of it. A knock on the portal caught her attention. She spoke the word to open it. Shev'la stood there more serious than before.

"Mareenth, I have just spoken with father. We must make haste and prepare to leave by night's beginning."

"I do not want to leave this place," she said.

"We have talked about this before," he said. "There is no telling what Zorath will do. It is certain that he will remember his town. Father thinks Zorath will decimate this place and everyone here."

"If he is so interested in taking Seranor, why does he take even a moment's interest in a town of nothing?"

"He is not rational—"

"He is most rational, most intelligent, and most capable. I cannot understand why he takes any interest in us."

"I do not know. Father knows more than me and he fears this more than anything. Will you do this for me?"

"Shev—"

"I love you so, Mareenth. I agree that we must leave. Without you in my life, I could not bear it."

"You have grown here, Shev. I can understand that you are willing to leave. I am not like this. This is my home. I have no interest to go anywhere else."

"Mareenth, please. Time is short. We must prepare. I will go to see father again and help him to pack things. Do not divulge this to anyone. No one knows about what we are doing in fear of Zorath releasing his anger sooner than expected plus many of the members would not want to leave."

"Such as me."

"But you are in danger if at all connected to my father. He worries daily about this. I will come back soon. Please, prepare. Once we are safe we can find a new town. I promise. And we can bear some seeds."

Mareenth turned to the painting she still held in her hands and once again focused on that determined look in Shev'la. She heard her husband leave by the faint closing of the portal at the front of the residence.

Chapter 17

ENTANS WERE really complex pieces of information. Organic messages bound in ceramic structure so that the message would not so easily disintegrate. Messages were composed and sent into the world so that a coherent theme might be found. Four-dimensional messages. The entan message contained the basis of creation, development and experiential learning devised by the hand of greater gods for the sole purpose of continued proliferation to reach the goal of the ultimate organic superstructure.

Tulai had studied the Kozotal 800 tios ago and learned of their flammic bodies traveling great distances without device, but he knew that there was a connection between flamma and the sending of objects and so spent many nights away from Calillian focused on his own desires. There was a desire in him to move quickly from one place to the next and so he experimented with flamma to test its ability to transfer more than just information which most arvatists were proficient in. His first wife did not seem to mind at the time though now that he reconsidered his actions he could remember her becoming more easily agitated, distanced and more focused on their seed Calil, whom he disregarded on an increasing basis. The rapid discoveries Tulai made in flamma travel blinded him to his wife's illness and later he could not prevent her death. Nor could he return her to the way she was and so improvised. How he missed her presence now.

Tulai removed the last arc-shaped piece of an 8-piece ceramic set and had strewn them about the floor. None had seen this before. It was one of Tulai's earlier works after he and Lez-win joined, and he became inspired one night by the clarity of an idea which previously only worked in theory and not in production. Organic flamma travel was made possible, via a circular flamma port, days later. Organic message travel.

The distracted inventor was too wrapped up in organizing his things and making preparations that he did not notice his first seedling's brooding entrance. Calil walked in a slow and measured pace. At about five meters distance he stopped and called out, "Father, we must talk!" Tulai turned around, semi-surprised to find Calil here and worried that Zorath was with him. After not seeing the Nivian nor feeling his presence so close he calmed and concerned himself with his seed.

"Why have you come, Calil?" asked Tulai.

"Father, you have wronged in your ways," started Calil, a tense and solemn face. "You have neglected me a whole life and in this neglect you have stolen my life and replaced it with a pain so deep that I am loathe to think of." He clanged uneasily on his suit of armor and a dwindling ring sounded.

"Calil, you are now part of Zorath. He has taken away the opus balance inside of you and replaced it with rigidity."

Each time the armored Calil spoke he stepped forward. "You talk of *balance* as it is something you know well."

"I have only given the nature of opus to you even if you failed to see it. My work is my life but I have loved all my family just the same," said father to seed.

"If there was one thing that I did not care for, it was your work. Your inventions have meant nothing to me," Calil replied.

"But they are for Seranor and those who live here."

"For Seranor – a dead planet – you would do so much, and for your seed you would take so much. This is not the action of a father. It is the action of an assassin."

"And what of your action today?" asked Tulai.

"What of it?" said Calil, defending his presence here.

"You did not come here to talk, did you?"

"I came here to remove bad memories that are hurting me inside." In a sudden spring forward, Calil withdrew his rader aiming it straight for his father's throat. Tulai managed a spell to deflect the quattro-blades away and was caught by Calil's knee that downed him. Calil moved the blades to his father's neck.

"Now, you must face the pain, father. You will know my pain, what I have felt my whole life."

"I was not against you before, Calil, as I am not against you now," heavy breaths came from the out-of-shape inventor. "Zorath has tainted your cerbind with things unspeakable." Tulai moved his hand, calling a command that sent Calil flying into the ceiling of the chamber. The fighter managed to land safely on his feet, a little disoriented from the crash at the top. The arvician spoke another and Calil's rader disintegrated in a cloud of moisture.

"I am your father! I will always be your father, Calil. I do not wish to hurt you but you must leave now!" Tulai prepared another spell this time a more brilliant white.

Calil withdrew a long dagger from his sheath and screamed "Die!" as he charged his father again who released his spell onto Calil's body. All things on him and near him began to be repelled until his clothes were thrown off and he could no longer pick up any sort of weapon. Calil ran around haphazardly and all material objects of reasonable size were repelled. The harder he tried the greater the disappointment. Calil became desperate to no avail.

"I have made your body resistant to all things material. Now leave before I go further!" said father to seed.

The angered seed jerked around trying to grab a weapon, even to get close enough to his father, without effect. "Father!" he screamed. "What have you done to me, father? You have taken everything away from me—from my life!" Not being able to touch or grab anything, Calil ran out the portal teary-eyed and naked as the day he was born. Tulai removed the spell he had just cast, but he could not remove the guilt he felt for what he had done.

CALIL RAN down the street not knowing where to go then saw a familiar face in the distance. It was Shev'la, his brother; he was waving his arms up and down while running in his direction. Calil recalled the joys they shared as youngsters and did not see Raskavron in full step, directly behind him. Shev'la was trying to warn him. The first blow sent Calil flying some ten meters to the left into a wall breaking his left leg. The second thrust threw him into the opposite wall across the street shattering his leg this time and forcing his right arm through the wall to leave him hanging there crippled and vulnerable like a doll in its master's hands. Raskavron then prepared an attack.

Tulai had become so hurt at what he had just done to his seed that he did not pick up right away on the arvic pulse of the Malkar but once he did he ran outside into the street. Shev'la had nearly arrived at the location all the while screaming. Tulai was still too far to have any effect; immediately, he flashed over. By the time he arrived Raskavron cast out shards of sharp ice that pierced every part of Calil's helpless nude body.

Shev'la jumped in, bastion in hand, and struck. The weapon bounced off the thick plates. Raskavron turned to his new attacker and created a sphere filled with liquid ice around Shev'la who began to die quickly. A brilliant light passed through the Malkar that seared a round hole from one end of him out the other end. Raskavron turned and sent out a wave of sub-zero liquid from his fists that Tulai shielded himself against before landing directly in front of him. He knew that he could not beat a Malkar in hand-to-hand combat so had to rely on his spells to destabilize him. He glanced over at Calil, impaled by a hundred spikes, who was now certainly dead before calling forth another more powerful spell. Then he saw Shev'la freezing to death and he acted. The ground beneath Raskavron melted pulling him down fully into it before the hard crust of the land was covered again leaving no sign of the Malkar. Another spell warmed the fluid bubble Shev'la was in, enough for him to break free. Tulai was sweating by the time that Shev'la was completely out, he had also retrieved Calil. Many Seronians now gathered in the streets worried about what was happening.

Many more angry footsteps were coming from behind them.

"We leave now! Get Mareenth and meet me at the back of our residence!" Shev'la did not have time to respond.

He touched his brother on the face. "Do not be angry, Calil. You did well. You have done what you wanted, isn't that right?" he asked knowing that there would be no response.

"Shev! Go! Fly like Nata!" yelled Tulai, again, this time pulling his seed away. Shev'la first walked backwards, noticed three figures walking in unison before running off to get his wife. Three drops of red tears left the ground stained beneath his feet.

In the background, milky bodies fell to the ground and some exploded in noxy fires. Hundreds of angry Seronians charged the philosophical few. A nearby square was littered with the dead and the dying. One entan, missing one eye and several fingers of his left hand, was giving a speech about the philosophy of love. It lasted a full eight minutes before a batier was impaled into him and podium.

Tulai stood by his seed's side momentarily before saying, "It is my fault that you were disillusioned. Sleep well my seed, be once again with your mother and know that your father loved you though he did not show it." He did not notice the three figures who came unannounced. Amid, Yano and Polinatum arrived in confident strides. They had been alerted by the actions of the Malkar.

"It must end today, Tulai," said Amid. "There have been enough deaths." A large commotion rang out about the town. Entans fought with entans. "Can you hear what has happened? The Nivian has washed his psychotic thoughts in our mud. Entans kill entans."

Tulai lay down his seed's head and stared at his Sagmal friend. "You have come to end it?" He did not care anymore.

"Yes," said Polinatum. "You mustn't involve yourself anymore. Take Shev'la and Mareenth to safety before more die. Zorath is near."

Tulai walked off several steps then stopped. "He cannot die, you know."

"Who?"

"The Nivian Zorath. He cannot die." Then he walked out of sight.

Tulai was nearly prepared by the time Shev'la and Mareenth arrived. He carried a large backpack stuffed with manuscripts and several oddly-shaped devices. Mareenth did not have time for any sort of rational decision. Shev'la just told her to leave with him and the two ran back to the unamid to join with his father.

"Tulai, what is happening?" she asked, impatiently, not satisfied up until now. Shev'la would not say anything more than Zorath had gone berserk and they were all in danger.

Tulai did not answer.

"I told you, Mareenth. We are leaving," said Shev'la.

"But why? What has happened?" she asked.

"Calil is dead. Zorath wants all those in Ulaq dead, especially my father!"

"Enough talk. Move!" Tulai said while putting the eight ceramic pieces together to form a circle outside in the back of the chamber. "Zorath will come and with the rod will destroy all that is. We must go. Amid, Polinatum and Yano have come to fight Zorath—"

"Father, they can fight him?"

"No. They will lose—Now let's fly!" He finished placing all the pieces together. "Step inside. Our time is shorter than we can imagine." He waved a pair of spells over them before activating the flamma port. A series of glyphs lit up, whispered weak tones and activated the superior technology. The three were recomposed into a message and, once ready, it was sent off far from its current location. Message sent.

RASKAVRON BURST out of its confines, in rage, and attacked the three for two rounds of damage to the environment before a thick red tail wrapped itself around Raskavron and he went flying through a wall. Panzor the Serag had arrived. Four arms and a large tail made up the ten meter creature.

"Panzor, the malkar must be exterminated for Seranor's sake," said Polinatum.

"Panzor will eat the vile and defecate his elemental existence!" roared Panzor. The Serag leaped into the building.

Zorath had watched from afar and after seeing what happened to Raskavron he flashed himself to the center of the battle scene. The three arvicians had already prepared for this situation and formed together in feromentan. Once the Nivian landed in the ideal range they joined their spell and cast it out at the unsuspecting Zorath. The phosphorescent fire of arvicity sprang out and encircled Blue Skin. Zorath struggled with it, even dropping Seca, as three focused against one. The background was filled with violence and commotion, but none ventured close to the four powerful beings at its center. A rainbow of colors flew like waves in the air. Some entans entered the strangely colored air and as they did their skin became warped before finally melting into liquid ceramic. Small mounds of entan goo could be seen.

Minutes dripped away and the enemy weakened. Amid was becoming weak himself from the strain, and Zorath caught this obscurity and exposed it with a spell made to disengage him. He succeeded. Amid fell by the wayside and the white arvic fire dissipated. Seca returned to his hand and before another action was made Yano was left for porcelan dust particles. Amid flashed, batier gleaming, and struck at the Nivian's neck as Polinatum worked a spell. Zorath deflected the spell but missed the black batier on his icy flesh. The batier cut clean through and dismembered his blue head.

Just as Amid was looking a Polinatum with the beginnings of a smile, an orange glow overtook him and his body, and his physical structure melted like snow to noxy fire. It was enough to surprise the Sagmal, who by now was the only one standing of

the original trio. Polinatum heard the final roar of
Panzor's voice from far behind and knew that their
plan had failed more miserably than the miserable
realm they opened. And he was at his weakest.
Zorath, headless and all, stood up to retrieve his
head. Placed it on his exposed neck and, head and
body, were rejoined. When he was done, Polinatum
had disappeared. Raskavron returned victoriously.
After all, this was a pure Malkar, the most potent of
all.

"Now, Tulai and all members will die," said
Zorath. Raskavron cast out a sheet of burning liquid
ice onto a hoard of ceramin on the street burning
and killing them. Zorath ran over to Tulai's
chamber, not satisfied he ran out to the back of the
unamid to find the large ceramic ring on the grass
floor and not a sign of Tulai. He waved his right
hand to learn of the secrets the ring or the area
contained. Everything left an arvic print with a
clear memory, but there was no memory that anyone
was here. The memory had been formatted and left
devoid of any information even to Zorath. He
snickered at Tulai's genius then frowned.

Up into the sky Zorath flew brandishing Seca –
carver of planets – and he called forth her energy to
cut the land and to soothe his hideous ferocity.
Bright rays of flamma came out of the white ball and
struck the land from all sides. The town's screams
of sheer agony were drowned in a phosphorescent
bubble. Other Seronians from several towns away
saw the bright light and it blinded those who looked

at it without protection. A sign that the end had come.

When everything had settled, the entire town had been decimated. Nothing remained but a deep crater. Zorath moved to the edge. He stood and stared at the emptiness for several hours all the while trying to conceive a resolution. So many things, so much has happened, so many deaths. What troubled him the most was that this gave him a good feeling, against what Seronians had taught him upon his resurrection. It felt good to be in control. To demonstrate one's politic and power.

Raskavron had partially filled it with putrid liquid and casually swam inside.

"Welcome to Lake Tulai," Zorath quietly said with no one to reply except an echo. No more shall I listen to the pathetic whims of this planet and its sub optimal beings. I have paid for my ignorance. To think that I could be together with entans is sheer folly. We are worlds apart. What will this planet do for me? And there are things that they must do. They will feed my lust and invigorate my plan against the Versos. My twin brother shall see me once again when his kol is wound up into my hand and wiped clean.

"Come, Raskavron! We will go to the Nivata mountains and create an army that will be the end of these beings."

"End of beings," said Raskavron, chugging the liquid. "Being the end."